RUTH RENDELL

THE FEVER TREE
AND OTHER STORIES OF SUSPENSE

Also by Ruth Rendell
Published by Ballantine Books:

TO FEAR A PAINTED DEVIL

VANITY DIES HARD

THE SECRET HOUSE OF DEATH

FROM DOON WITH DEATH

SINS OF THE FATHERS

WOLF TO THE SLAUGHTER

THE BEST MAN TO DIE

A GUILTY THING SURPRISED

DEATH NOTES

MASTER OF THE MOOR

THE FEVER TREE

AND OTHER STORIES OF SUSPENSE

RUTH RENDELL

BALLANTINE BOOKS • NEW YORK

Originally published in Great Britain by Hutchinson & Co.

Copyright © 1982 by Kingsmarkham Enterprises, Ltd.

Author's Note
The following stories have already appeared in *Ellery Queen's Mystery Magazine*:

The Fever Tree; A Glowing Future (published under the title 'A Present for Patricia'); An Outside Interest (published under the title 'The Man Who Frightened Women'); A Case of Coincidence; Thornapple (published under the title 'The Boy Who Collected Poison'); May and June (published under the title 'The Strong and the Weak'); A Needle for the Devil; Front Seat (published under the title 'Truth Will Out'); Paintbox Place (published under the title 'The Paintbox Houses'); The Wrong Category (published under the title 'On the Path')

Library of Congress Catalog Card Number: 82-19014

ISBN 0-345-31069-1

This edition published by arrangement with Pantheon Books

Manufactured in the United States of America
First Ballantine Books Edition: January 1984

Contents

For Catherine, Pam and Brett Jones

The Fever Tree

Where malaria is, there grows the fever tree.

It has the feathery fern-like leaves, fresh green and tender, that are common to so many trees in tropical regions. Its shape is graceful with an air of youth, as if every fever tree is still waiting to grow up. But the most distinctive thing about it is the colour of its bark which is the yellow of an unripe lemon. The fever trees stand out from among the rest because of their slender yellow trunks.

Ford knew what the tree was called and he could recognize it but he didn't know what its botanical name was. Nor had he ever heard why it was called the fever tree, whether the tribesmen used its leaves or bark or fruit as a specific against malaria or if it simply took its name from its warning presence wherever the malaria-carrying mosquito was. The sight of it in Ntsukunyane seemed to promote a fever in his blood.

An African in khaki shorts and shirt lifted up the bar for them so that their car could pass through the opening in the fence. Inside it looked no different from outside, the same bush, still, silent, unstirred by wind, stretching away on

either side. Ford, driving the two miles along the tarmac
road to the reception hut, thought of how it would be if he
turned his head and saw Marguerite in the passenger seat beside him. It was an illusion he dared not have but was allowed to keep for only a minute. Tricia shattered it. She began to belabour him with schoolgirl questions, uttered in a
bright and desperate voice.

Another African, in a fancier, more decorated uniform,
took their booking voucher and checked it against a ledger.
You had to pay weeks in advance for the privilege of staying
here. Ford had booked the day after he had said goodbye to
Marguerite and returned, for ever, to Tricia.

'My wife wants to know the area of Ntsukunyane,' he
said.

'Four million acres.'

Ford gave the appropriate whistle. 'Do we have a chance
of seeing a leopard?'

The man shrugged, smiled, 'Who knows? You may be
lucky. You're here a whole week so you should see lion, elephant, hippo, cheetah maybe. But the leopard is nocturnal
and you must be back in camp by six p.m.' He looked at his
watch. 'I advise you to get on now, sir, if you're to make
Thaba before they close the gates.'

Ford got back into the car. It was nearly four. The sun of
Africa, a living presence, a personal god, burned through a
net of haze. There was no wind. Tricia, in a pale yellow
sundress with frills, had hung her arm outside the open window and the fair downy skin was glowing red. He told her
what the man had said and he told her about the notice
pinned inside the hut: *It is strictly forbidden to bring fire-
arms into the game reserve, to feed the animals, to exceed
the speed limit, to litter.*

'And most of all you mustn't get out of the car,' said
Ford.

'What, not ever?' said Tricia, making her pale blue eyes
round and naive and marble-like.

'That's what it says.'

She pulled a face. 'Silly old rules!'

'They have to have them,' he said.

In here as in the outside world. It is strictly forbidden to fall in love, to leave your wife, to try to begin anew. He glanced at Tricia to see if the same thoughts were passing through her mind. Her face wore its arch expression, winsome.

'A prize,' she said, 'for the first one to see an animal.'

'All right.' He had agreed to this reconciliation, to bring her on this holiday, this second honeymoon, and now he must try. He must work at it. It wasn't just going to happen as love had sprung between him and Marguerite, unsought and untried for. 'Who's going to award it?' he said.

'You are if it's me and I am if it's you. And if it's me I'd like a presey from the camp shop. A very nice pricey presey.'

Ford was the winner. He saw a single zebra come out from among the thorn trees on the right-hand side, then a small herd. 'Do I get a present from the shop?'

He could sense rather than see her shake her head with calculated coyness. 'A kiss,' she said and pressed warm dry lips against his cheek.

It made him shiver a little. He slowed down for the zebra to cross the road. The thorn bushes had spines on them two inches long. By the roadside grew a species of wild zinnia with tiny flowers, coral red, and these made red drifts among the coarse pale grass. In the bush were red ant hills with tall peaks like towers on a castle in a fairy story. It was thirty miles to Thaba. He drove on just within the speed limit, ignoring Tricia as far as he could whenever she asked him to slow down. They weren't going to see one of the big predators, anyway not this afternoon, he was certain of that, only impala and zebra and maybe a giraffe. On business trips in the past he'd taken time off to go to Serengeti and Kruger and he knew. He got the binoculars out for Tricia and adjusted them and hooked them round her neck, for he hadn't forgotten the binoculars and cameras she had dropped and smashed in the past through failing to do that, and her tears afterwards. The car wasn't air-conditioned and the heat lay heavy and still between them. Ahead of them, as they drove westwards, the sun was sinking in a dull yellow glare. The sweat flowed out of Ford's armpits and between his shoulder blades, soaking his already wet shirt and laying a cold sticky film on his skin.

A stone pyramid with arrows on it, set in the middle of a junction of roads, pointed the way to Thaba, to the main camp at Waka-suthu and to Hippo Bridge over the Suthu River. On top of it sat a baboon with her grey fluffy infant on her knees. Tricia yearned for it, stretching out her arms. She had never had a child. The baboon began picking fleas out of its baby's scalp. Tricia gave a little nervous scream, half-disgusted, half-joyful. Ford drove down the road to Thaba and in through the entrance to the camp ten minutes before they closed the gates for the night.

The dark comes down fast in Africa. Dusk is of short duration; no sooner have you noticed it than it has gone and night has fallen. In the few moments of dusk, pale things glimmer brightly and birds make a soft murmuring. In the camp at Thaba were a restaurant and a shop, round huts with thatched roofs and wooden chalets with porches. Ford and Tricia had been assigned a chalet on the northern perimeter and from their porch, beyond the high, wire fence, you could see the Suthu River flowing smoothly and silently between banks of tall reeds. Dusk had just come as they walked up the wooden steps, Ford carrying their cases. It was then that he saw the fever trees, two of them, their ferny leaves bleached to grey by the twilight but their trunks a sharper, stronger yellow than in the day.

'Just as well we took our anti-malaria pills,' said Ford as he pushed open the door. When the light was switched on he could see two mosquitoes on the opposite wall. 'Anopheles is the malaria carrier but unfortunately they don't announce whether they're anopheles or not.'

Twin beds, a table, lamps, an air conditioner, a fridge, a door, standing open, to lavatory and shower. Tricia dropped her make-up case, without which she went nowhere, on to the bed by the window. The light wasn't very bright. None of the lights in the camp were because the electricity came from a generator. They were a small colony of humans in a world that belonged to the animals, a reversal of the usual order of things. From the window you could see other chalets, other dim lights, other parked cars. Tricia talked to the two mosquitoes.

'Is your name Anna Phyllis? No. Darling, you're quite safe. She says she's Mary Jane and her husband's John Henry.'

Ford managed to smile. He had accepted and grown used to Tricia's facetiousness until he had encountered Marguerite's wit. He shoved his case, without unpacking it, into the cupboard and went to have a shower. Tricia stood on the porch, listening to the cicadas, thousands of them. It had gone pitch dark while she was hanging up her dresses and the sky was punctured all over with bright stars.

She had got Ford back from that woman and now she had to keep him. She had lost some weight, bought a lot of new clothes and had had highlights put in her hair. Men had always made her feel frightened, starting with her father when she was a child. It was then, when a child, that she had purposely began *playing* the child with its winning little ways. She had noticed that her father was kinder and more forbearing towards little girls than towards her mother. Ford had married a little girl, clinging and winsome, and had liked it well enough till he had met a grown woman. Tricia knew all that, but now she knew no better how to keep him than she did then; the old methods were as weary and stale to her as she guessed they might be to him. Standing there on the porch, she half-wished she were alone and didn't have to have a husband, didn't, for the sake of convention and of pride, for support and society, have to hold tight on to him. She listened wistfully for a lion to roar out there in the bush beyond the fence, but there was no sound except the cicadas.

Ford came out in a towelling robe. 'What did you do with the mosquito stuff? The spray?'

Frightened at once, she said, 'I don't know.'

'What do you mean, you don't know? You must know. I gave you the aerosol at the hotel and said to put it in that make-up case of yours.'

She opened the case, though she knew the mosquito stuff wasn't there. Of course it wasn't. She could see it on the bathroom shelf in the hotel, left behind because it was too bulky. She bit her lip, looked sideways at Ford. 'We can get some more at the shop.'

'Tricia, the shop closes at seven and it's now ten past.'

'We can get some in the morning.'

'Mosquitoes happen to be most active at night.' He rummaged among the bottles and jars in the case. 'Look at all this useless rubbish. "Skin cleanser", "pearlized foundation", "moisturizer" — like some young model girl. I suppose it didn't occur to you to bring the anti-mosquito spray and leave the "pearlized foundation" behind.'

Her lip trembled. She could feel herself, almost involuntarily, rounding her eyes, forming her mouth into the shape for lisping. 'We did 'member to take our pills.'

'That won't stop the damn' things biting.' He went back into the shower and slammed the door.

Marguerite wouldn't have forgotten to bring that aerosol. Tricia knew he was thinking of Marguerite again, that his head was full of her, that she had entered his thoughts powerfully and insistently on the long drive to Thaba. She began to cry. The water went on running out of her eyes and wouldn't stop, so she changed her dress while she cried and the tears came through the powder she put on her face.

They had dinner in the restaurant. Tricia, in pink flow-ered crepe, was the only dressed-up woman there, and while once she would have fancied the other diners looked at her in admiration now she thought it must be with derision. She ate her small piece of overcooked hake and her large piece of overcooked, breadcrumbed veal, and watched the red weals from mosquito bites coming up on Ford's arms.

There were no lights on in the camp but those which shone from the windows of the main building and from the chalets. Gradually the lights went out and it became very dark. In spite of his mosquito bites, Ford fell asleep at once but the noise of the air-conditioning kept Tricia awake. At eleven she switched it off and opened the window. Then she did sleep but she awoke again at four, lay awake for half an hour, got up and put her clothes on and went out.

It was still dark but the darkness was lifting as if the thickest veil of it had been withdrawn. A heavy dew lay on the grass. As she passed under the merula tree, laden with small green apricot-shaped fruits, a flock of bats flew out from its branches and circled her head. If Ford had been with her she would have screamed and clung to him but be-cause she was alone she kept silent. The camp and the bush beyond the fence were full of sound. The sounds brought to Tricia's mind the paintings of Hieronymus Bosch, imps and demons and dreadful homunculi which, if they had uttered, might have made noises like these, gruntings and soft whis-tles and chirps and little thin squeals.

She walked about, waiting for the dawn, expecting it to come with drama. But it was only a grey pallor in the sky, a paleness between parting black clouds, and the feeling of let-down frightened her as if it were a symbol or an omen of something more significant in her life than the coming of morning.

Ford woke up, unable at first to open his eyes for the swelling from mosquito bites. There were mosquitoes like threads of thistledown on the walls, all over the walls. He

got up and staggered, half-blind, out of the bedroom and let
the water from the shower run on his eyes. Tricia came and
stared at his face, giggling nervously and biting her lip.

The camp gates opened at five-thirty and the cars began
their exodus. Tricia had never passed a driving test and Ford
couldn't see, so they went to the restaurant for breakfast instead. When the shop opened Ford bought two kinds of
mosquito repellant and, impatiently, because he could no
longer bear her apologies and her pleading eyes, a necklace
of ivory beads for Tricia and a skirt with giraffes printed on
it. At nine o'clock, when the swelling round Ford's eyes had
subsided a little, they set off in the car, taking the road for
Hippo Bridge.

The day was humid and thickly hot. Ford had counted the
number of mosquito bites he had and the total was twenty-
four. It was hard to believe that two little tablets of quinine
would be proof against twenty-four bites, some of which
must certainly have been inflicted by anopheles. Hadn't he
seen the two fever trees when they arrived last night? Now
he drove the car slowly and doggedly, hardly speaking, his
swollen eyes concealed behind sunglasses. By the Suthu
River and then by a water hole he stopped and they watched.
But they saw nothing come to the water's edge unless you
counted the log which at last disappeared, thus proving itself
to have been a crocodile. It was too late in the morning to
see much apart from the marabou storks which stood one-
legged, still and hunched, in a clearing or on the gaunt
branch of a tree. Through binoculars Ford stared at the bush
which stretched in unbroken, apparently untenanted, same-
ness to the blue ridge of mountains on the far horizon.

There could be no real fever from the mosquito bites. If
malaria were to come it wouldn't be yet. But Ford, sitting in
the car beside Tricia, nevertheless felt something like a de-
lirium of fever. It came perhaps from the gross irritation of
the whole surface of his body, from the tender burning of his
skin and from his inability to move without setting up fresh

torment. It affected his mind too, so that each time he looked at Tricia a kind of panic rose in him. Why had he done it? Why had he gone back to her? Was he mad? His eyes and his head throbbed as if his temperature was raised. Tricia's pink jeans were too tight for her and the frills on her white voile blouse ridiculous. With the aid of the binoculars she had found a family of small grey monkeys in the branches of a peepul tree and she was cooing at them out of the window. Presently she opened the car door, held it just open and turned to look at him the way a child looks at her father when he has forbidden something she nevertheless longs and means to do.

They hadn't had sight of a big cat or an elephant, they hadn't even seen a jackal. Ford lifted his shoulders.

'O.K. But if a ranger comes along and catches you we'll be in dead trouble.'

She got out of the car, leaving the door open. The grass which began at the roadside and covered the bush as far as the eye could see was long and coarse. It came up above Tricia's knees. A lioness or a cheetah lying in it would have been entirely concealed. Ford picked up the binoculars and looked the other way to avoid watching Tricia who had once again forgotten to put the camera strap round her neck. She was making overtures to the monkeys who shrank away from her, embracing each other and burying heads in shoulders, like menaced refugees in a sentimental painting. He moved the glasses slowly. About a hundred yards from where a small herd of buck grazed uneasily, he saw the two cat faces close together, the bodies nestled together, the spotted backs. Cheetah. It came into his mind how he had heard that they were the fastest animals on earth.

He ought to call to Tricia and get her back at once into the car. He didn't call. Through the glasses he watched the big cats that reclined there so gracefully, satiated, at rest, yet with open eyes. Marguerite would have liked them, she loved cats, she had a Burmese, as lithe and slim and poised as one of these wild creatures. Tricia got back into the car, exclaiming how sweet the monkeys were. He started the car and drove off without saying anything to her about the chee- tahs.

Later, at about five in the afternoon, she wanted to get out of the car again and he didn't stop her. She walked up and down the road, talking to mongooses. In something over an hour it would be dark. Ford imagined starting up the car and driving back to the camp without her. Leopards were noc- turnal hunters, waiting till dark. The swelling around his eyes had almost subsided now but his neck and arms and hands ached from the stiffness of the bites. The mongooses fled into the grass as Tricia approached, whispering to them, hands outstretched. A car with four men in it was coming along from the Hippo Bridge direction. It slowed down and the driver put his head out. His face was brick-red, thick- featured, his hair corrugated blond, and his voice had the squashed vowels accent of the white man born in Africa.

'The lady shouldn't be out on the road like that.'

'I know,' said Ford. 'I've told her.'

'Excuse me, d'you know you're doing a very dangerous thing, leaving your car?' The voice had a hectoring boom. Tricia blushed. She bridled, smiled, bit her lip, though she was in fact very afraid of this man who was looking at her as if he despised her, as if she disgusted him. When he got back to camp, would he betray her?

'Promise you won't tell on me?' she faltered, her head on one side.

He gave an exclamation of anger and withdrew his head. The car moved forward. Tricia gave a skip and a jump into the passenger seat beside Ford. They had under an hour in which to get back to Thaba. Ford drove back, following the car with the four men in it.

At dinner they sat at adjoining tables. Tricia wondered how many people they had told about her, for she fancied that some of the diners looked at her with curiosity or antagonism. The man with fair curly hair they called Eric boasted loudly of what he and his companions had seen that day, a whole pride of lions, two rhinoceros, hyena and the rare sable antelope.

'You can't expect to see much down that Hippo Bridge road, you know,' he said to Ford. 'All the game's up at Sotingwe. You take the Sotingwe road first thing tomorrow and I'll guarantee you lions.'

He didn't address Tricia, he didn't even look at her. Ten years before, men in restaurants had turned their heads to look at her and though she had feared them, she had basked, trembling, in their gaze. Walking across the grass, back to their chalet, she held on to Ford's arm.

'For God's sake, mind my mosquito bites,' said Ford.

He lay awake a long while in the single bed a foot away from Tricia's, thinking about the leopard out there beyond the fence that hunted at night. The leopard would move along the branch of a tree and drop upon its prey. Lionesses hunted in the early morning and brought the kill to their mate and the cubs. Ford had seen all that sort of thing on television. How cheetahs hunted he didn't know except that they were very swift. An angry elephant would lean on a car and crush it or smash a windscreen with a blow from its foot. It was too dark for him to see Tricia but he knew she was awake, lying still, sometimes holding her breath. He heard her breath released in an exhalation, a sigh, that was audible above the rattle of the air-conditioner.

Years ago he had tried to teach her to drive. They said a husband should never try to teach his wife, he would have no patience with her and make no allowances. Tricia's progress had never been maintained, she had always been liable to do silly reckless things and then he had shouted at her. She took a driving test and failed and she said this was because the examiner had bullied her. Tricia seemed to think no one should ever raise his voice to her, and at one glance from her all men should fall slaves at her feet.

He would have liked her to be able to take a turn at driving. There was no doubt you missed a lot when you had to concentrate on the road. But it was no use suggesting it. Theirs was one of the first cars in the line to leave the gates at five-thirty, to slip out beyond the fence into the grey dawn, the still bush. At the stone pyramid, on which a family of baboons sat clustered, Ford took the road for Sotingwe.

A couple of miles up they came upon the lions. Eric and his friends were already there, leaning out of the car windows with cameras. The lions, two full-grown lionesses, two lioness cubs and a lion cub with his mane beginning to sprout, were lying on the roadway. Ford stopped and parked the car on the opposite side to Eric.

'Didn't I say you'd be lucky up here?' Eric called to Tricia, 'Not got any ideas about getting out and investigating, I hope.'

Tricia didn't answer him or look at him. She looked at the lions. The sun was coming up, radiating the sky with a pinkish-orange glow and a little breeze fluttered all the pale green, fern-like leaves. The larger of the adult lionesses, bored rather than alarmed by Eric's elaborate photographic equipment, got up slowly and strolled into the bush, in among the long dry grass and the red zinnias. The cubs followed her, the other lioness followed her. Through his binoculars Ford watched them stalk with proud, lifted heads, walking, even the little ones, in a graceful, measured, controlled way. There were no impala anywhere, no giraffe, no wildebeest. The world here belonged to the lions.

All the game was gathered at Sotingwe, near the water hole. An elephant with ears like punkahs was powdering himself with red earth blown out through his trunk. Tricia got out of the car to photograph the elephant and Ford didn't try to stop her. He scratched his mosquito bites which had passed the burning and entered the itchy stage. Once more Tricia had neglected to pass the camera strap round her neck. She made her way down to the water's edge and stood at a safe distance — was it a safe distance? Was any distance safe in here? — looking at a crocodile. Ford thought, without really explaining to himself or even fully understanding what he meant, that it was the wrong time of day, it was too early. They went back to Thaba for breakfast.

At breakfast and again at lunch Eric was very full of what he had seen. He had taken the dirt road that ran down from Sotingwe to Suthu Bridge and there, up in a tree near the water, had been a leopard. Malcolm had spotted it first, stretched out asleep on a branch, a long way off but quite easy to see through field glasses.

'Massive great fella with your authentic square-type spots,' said Eric, smoking a cigar.

Tricia, of course, wanted to go to Suthu Bridge, so Ford took the dirt road after they had had their siesta. Malcolm described exactly where he had seen the leopard which might, for all he knew, still be sleeping on its branch.

'About half a mile up from the bridge. You look over on your left and there's a sort of clearing with one of those trees with yellow trunks in it. This chap was on a branch on the right side of the clearing.'

The dirt road was a track of crimson earth between green verges. Ford found the clearing with the single fever tree but the leopard had gone. He drove slowly down to the bridge that spanned the sluggish green river. When he switched off the engine it was silent and utterly still, the air hot and close, nothing moving but the mosquitoes that danced in their haphazard yet regular measure above the surface of the water.

Tricia was getting out of the car as a matter of course now. This time she didn't even trouble to give him the coy glance that asked permission. She was wearing a red and white striped sundress with straps that were too narrow and a skirt that was too tight. She ran down to the water's edge, took off a sandal and dipped in a daring foot. She laughed and twirled her feet, dabbling the dry round stones with water drops. Ford thought how he had loved this sort of thing when he had first met her, and now he was going to have to bear it for the rest of his life. He broke into a sweat as if his temperature had suddenly risen.

She was prancing about on the stones and in the water, holding up her skirt. There were no animals to be seen. All afternoon they had seen nothing but impala, and the sun was moving down now, beginning to colour the hazy, pastel sky. Tricia, on the opposite bank, broke another Ntsukunyane rule and picked daisies, tucking one behind each ear. With a flower between her teeth like a Spanish dancer, she swayed her hips and smiled.

Ford turned the ignition key and started the car. It would be dark in just over an hour and long before that they would have closed the gates at Thaba. He moved the car forward, reversed, making what Tricia, no doubt, would call a three-point turn. Facing towards Thaba now, he put the selector into drive, his foot on the accelerator, he took a deep breath as the sweat trickled between his shoulder blades. The heat made mirages on the road and out of them a car was coming. Ford stopped and switched off the engine. It wasn't Eric's car but one belonging to a couple of young Americans on holiday. The boy raised his hand in a salute at Ford.

Ford called out to Tricia, 'Come on or we'll be late.' She got into the car, dropping her flowers on to the roadway. Ford had been going to leave her there, that was how much he wanted to be rid of her. Her body began to shake and she clasped her hands tightly together so that he shouldn't see. He had been going to drive away and leave her there to the darkness and the lions, the leopard that hunted by night. He had been driving away, only the Americans' car had come along.

She was silent, thinking about it. The Americans turned back soon after they did and followed them up the dirt road. Impala stood around the solitary fever tree, listening perhaps to inaudible sounds or scenting invisible danger. The sky was smoky yellow with sunset. Tricia thought about what Ford must have intended to do, drive back to camp just before they closed the gates, watch the darkness come down, knowing she was out there, say not a word of her absence to anyone — and who would miss her? Eric? Malcolm? Ford wouldn't have gone to the restaurant and in the morning when they opened the gates he would have driven away. No need even to check out at Ntsukunyane where you paid weeks in advance.

The perfect murder. Who would search for her, not knowing there was need for search? And if her bones were found? One set of bones, human, impala, waterbuck, looks very much like another after the jackals have been at them and the vultures. And when he reached home he would have said he had left her for Marguerite. . .

He was nicer to her that evening, gentler. Because he was afraid she had guessed or might guess the truth of what had happened at Sotingwe?

'We said we'd have champagne one night. How about now? No time like the present.'

'If you like,' Tricia said. She felt sick all the time, she had no appetite.

Ford toasted them in champagne. 'To us!'

He ordered the whole gamut of the menu, soup, fish, Wiener schnitzel, *crème brûlée*. She picked at her food, thinking how he had meant to kill her. She would never be safe now, for having failed once he would try again. Not the same method perhaps but some other. How was she to know he hadn't already tried? Maybe, for instance, he had substituted aspirin for those quinine tablets, or when they were back in the hotel in Mombasa he might try to drown her. She would never be safe unless she left him.

Which was what he wanted, which would be the next best thing to her death. Lying awake in the night, she thought of what that would mean, going back to live with her mother while he went to Marguerite. He wasn't asleep either. She could hear the sound of his irregular wakeful breathing. She heard the bed creak as he moved in it restlessly, the air conditioning grinding, the whine of a mosquito. Now, if she hadn't already been killed she might be wandering out there in the bush, in terror in the dark, afraid to take a step but afraid to remain still, fearful of every sound yet not knowing which sound most to fear. There was no moon. She had taken note of that before she came to bed and had seen in her diary that tomorrow the moon would be new. The sky had been overcast at nightfall and now it was pitch dark. The leopard could see, perhaps by the light of the stars or with an inner instinctive eye more sure than simple vision and would drop silently from its branch to sink its teeth into the lifted throat.

The mosquito that had whined bit Ford in several places on his face and neck and on his left foot. He had forgotten to use the repellant the night before. Early in the morning, at dawn, he got up and dressed and went for a walk round the camp. There was no one about but one of the African staff, hosing down a guest's car. Squeaks and shufflings came from the bush beyond the fence.

Had he really meant to rid himself of Tricia by throwing her, as one might say, to the lions? For a mad moment, he supposed, because fever had got into his blood, poison into his veins. She knew, he could tell that. In a way it might be all to the good, her knowing, it would show her how hopeless the marriage was that she was trying to preserve.

The swellings on his foot, though covered by his sock, were making the instep bulge through the sandal. His foot felt stiff and burning and he became aware that he was limping slightly. Supporting himself against the trunk of a fever tree, his skin against its cool, dampish, yellow bark, he took off his sandal and felt his swollen foot tenderly with his fingertips. Mosquitoes never touched Tricia, they seemed to shirk contact with her pale dry flesh.

She was up when he hobbled in, she was sitting on her

bed, painting her fingernails. How could he live with a
woman who painted her fingernails in a game reserve?

They didn't go out till nine. On the road to Waka-suthu
Eric's car met them, coming back.

'There's nothing down there for miles, you're wasting
your time.'

'O.K.,' said Ford. 'Thanks.'

'Sotingwe's the place. Did you see the leopard yesterday?' Ford shook his head. 'Oh, well, we can't all be
lucky.'

Elephants were playing in the river at Hippo Bridge,
spraying each other with water and nudging heavy shoulders. Ford thought that was going to be the high spot of the
morning until they came upon the kill. They didn't actually
see it. The kill had taken place some hours before, but the
lioness and her cubs were still picking at the carcase, at a
blood-blackened rib cage. They sat in the car and watched.
After a while the lions left the carcase and walked away in
file through the grass, but the little jackals were already
gathered, a pack of them, posted behind trees. Ford came
back that way again at four and by then the vultures had
moved in, picking the bones.

It was a hot day of merciless sunshine, the sky blue and
perfectly clear. Ford's foot was swollen to twice its normal
size. He noticed that Tricia hadn't once left the car that day,
nor had she spoken girlishly to him or giggled or given him a
roguish kiss. She thought he had been trying to kill her, a
preposterous notion really. The truth was he had only been
giving her a fright, teaching her how stupid it was to flout
the rules and leave the car. Why should he kill her, anyway?
He could leave her, he *would* leave her, and once they were
back in Mombasa he would tell her so. The thought of it
made him turn to her and smile. He had stopped by the
clearing where the fever tree stood, yellow of bark, delicate
and fern-like of leaf, in the sunshine like a young sapling in
springtime.

'Why don't you get out any more?'

She faltered, 'There's nothing to see.'

'No?'

He had spotted the porcupine with his naked eye but he handed her the binoculars. She looked and laughed with pleasure. That was the way she used to laugh when she was young, not from amusement but delight. He shut his eyes. 'Oh, the sweetie porky-pine!'

She reached onto the back seat for the camera. And then she hesitated. He could see the fear, the caution in her eyes. Silently he took the key out of the ignition and held it out to her on the palm of his hand. She flushed. He stared at her, enjoying her discomfiture, indignant that she should suspect him of such baseness.

She hesitated but she took the key. She picked up the camera and opened the car door, holding the key by its fob in her left hand, the camera in her right. He noticed that she hadn't passed the strap of the camera, his treasured Pentax, round her neck, she never did. For the thousandth time he could have told her but he lacked the heart to speak. His swollen foot throbbed and he thought of the long days at Ntsukunyane that remained to them. Marguerite seemed infinitely far away, further even than at the other side of the world where she was.

He knew Tricia was going to drop the camera some fifteen seconds before she did so. It was because she had the key in her other hand. If the strap had been round her neck it wouldn't have mattered. He knew how it was when you held something in each hand and lost your grip or your footing. You had no sense then, in that instant, of which of the objects was valuable and mattered and which was not and didn't. Tricia held on to the key and dropped the camera. The better to photograph the porcupine, she had mounted on to the twisted roots of a tree, roots that looked as hard as a flight of stone steps.

She gave a little cry. At the sounds of the crash and the

cry the porcupine erected its quills. Ford jumped out of the car, wincing when he put his foot to the ground, hobbling through the grass to Tricia who stood as if petrified with fear of him. The camera, the pieces of camera, had fallen among the gnarled, stone-like tree roots. He dropped on to his knees, shouting at her, cursing her.

Tricia began to run. She ran back to the car and pushed the key into the ignition. The car was pointing in the direction of Thaba and the clock on the dashboard shelf said five thirty-five. Ford came limping back, waving his arms at her, his hands full of broken pieces of camera. She looked away and put her foot down hard on the accelerator.

The sky was clear orange with sunset, black bars of the coming night lying on the horizon. She found she could drive when she had to, even though she couldn't pass a test. A mile along the road she met the American couple. The boy put his head out. 'Anything worth going down there for?'

'Not a thing,' said Tricia, 'you'd be wasting your time.'

The boy turned his car and followed her back. It was two minutes past six when they entered Thaba, the last cars to do so. The gates closed behind them.

The Dreadful Day
of Judgement

There were four of them working in the cemetery. They
were employed by the city corporation — to do what? Even
the foreman was vague about their duties which had not
been very precisely specified. Not to clear the central part,
certainly, for that would have been a task not for four but for
four hundred. And a wild life sanctuary, for which purpose
it was designated, must be wild. To tidy it, then, to remove
the worst signs of vandalism, to carry away such gravestones as had fallen, to denude certain of the many winding
paths of the intrusive bramble and ivy and nettle. When they
asked the foreman whether this should be done or that, he
would say to use their own judgement, he couldn't be sure,
he would find out. But he never did. Sometimes an official
from the corporation came and viewed the work and nodded
and disappeared into the hut with the foreman to drink tea.
As the winter came on the official appeared less often, and
the foreman said it was a hopeless task, they needed more
men, but the corporation could no longer afford to spend the
money, they must just do the best they could.

The hut was just inside the main gates. The foreman had a

plan of the cemetery pinned to the wall next to Gilly's calendar of the girl in the transparent nightdress. He had a kettle and a spirit stove, but the cups and the teapot had been brought by Marlon who got them from his mother. The hut was always hot and smelly and smoky. The foreman chain-smoked and so did Marlon, although he was so young, and everywhere in the hut were saucers full of ash and cigarette stubs. One day Gilly, who didn't smoke, brought into the hut a tin can he had found in an open vault. The foreman and Marlon seemed pleased to have a new, clean ashtray, for they never considered emptying the others but let them fill up and spill about the floor.

'Marlon'd be scared stiff if he knew where that came from,' said John. 'He'd die of fright.'

But Gilly only laughed. He found everything about the cemetery funny, even the soldiers' graves, the only well-tended ones, that the Imperial War Graves Commission still looked after. In the beginning he had amused himself by jumping out on Marlon from behind a monument or a pillared tomb, but the foreman, lethargic as he was, had stopped that because Marlon was not quite as they were, being backward and not able to read or write much.

The main gates hung between what the foreman called stone posts but which John alone knew were Corinthian columns. A high wall surrounded the cemetery, which was of many acres, and the periphery of it, a wide space just inside the wall, had been cleared long before and turfed and planted with trees that were still tiny. This was to be a public park for the townsfolk. It was the centre, the deep heart of the place, once the necropolis for this mercantile city, that was to be left for the birds and such small animals who would venture in and stay.

Many species of bird already nested in the ilexes and the laurels, the elms and the thin, silver-trunked birch trees. Crows with wings like black fans, woodpeckers whose tap-tap-tapping could be heard from the almost impenetrable depths, little birds which even John couldn't name and which crept rather than hopped over the lichen on the fallen stones. It was silent in there but for the rare rustle of wings or the soft crack of a decayed twig dropping. The city lay below, all round, but in winter it was often masked by fog, and it was hard to believe that thousands lived down there and worked and scurried in glare and noise. Their forbears' tombs stood in rows or gathered in clusters or jostled each other haphazardly: domed follies, marble slabs, granite crosses, broken columns, draped urns, simple stones, all overgrown and shrouded and half-obscured. Not a famous name among them, not a memorable title, only the obscure dead, forgotten, abandoned, capable now of nothing more than to decree a hush.

The silence was violated only by Gilly's talk. He had one topic of conversation, but that one was inexhaustible and everything recalled him to it. A name on a tomb, a scrap of verse on a gravestone, a pair of sparrows, the decorously robed statue of an angel. 'Bit of all right, that one,' he would say, stroking the stone flesh of a weeping muse, his hands so coarse and calloused that John wondered how any real woman could bear them to touch her. Or, lifting the ivy from a grave where lay a matron who had married three times, 'Couldn't get enough of it, could she?' And these reflections led him into endless reminiscences of the women he had had, those he now possessed, and anticipations of those awaiting him in the future.

Nothing stayed him. Not the engraved sorrow of parents mourning a daughter dead at seventeen, not the stone evocations of the sufferings of those dead in childbirth. Some of the vaults had been despoiled and left open, and he would penetrate them, descending subterranean stairs, shouting up to John and Marlon from the depths that here was a good place to bring a girl. 'Be O.K. in the summer. There's shelves here, make a good bed, they would. Proper little boudoir.'

John often regretted the thing he had done which made Gilly admire him. It had been on his first day there. He knew, even before he had done it, that this was to show them he was different from them, to make it clear from the start that he was a labourer only because there was no other work obtainable for such as he. He wanted them to know he had been to a university and was a qualified teacher. The shame and humiliation of being forced to take this unskilled work ate into his soul. They must understand his education had fitted him for something higher. But it had been a foolish vanity.

There had been nothing in the deep cavity any more but stones and dead leaves. But he had jumped in and held up a big pitted stone and cried ringingly: 'That skull had a tongue in it and could sing once. How the knave jowls it to the ground, as if 'twere Cain's jawbone that did the first murder!'

Gilly stared. 'You make that up yourself?'

'Shakespeare,' he said. 'Hamlet,' and the awe on Gilly's unformed pug-nosed face made him go on, excited with success, a braggart in a squalid pit. 'Prithee, Horatio, tell me one thing. Dost thou think Alexander looked o' this fashion i' the earth? And smelt so? pah!'

Marlon had gone white, his face peaked between the falls of thin yellow hair. He wore a heavy blue garment, a kind of anorak, but it gave him a medieval look standing there against the chapel wall, an El Greco sky flowing above its tower, purple and black and rushing in scuds above this northern Toledo. But Gilly was laughing, begging John to go on, and John went on, playing to the groundlings, holding the stone aloft. 'Alas, poor Yorick. . .' until at last he flung it from him with the ham actor's flourish, and up on the path again was being clapped on the back by Gilly and told what a brain he'd got. And Gilly was showing what he was and what all that had meant to him by demanding to

have that bit again, the bit about the lips that I have kissed I
know not how oft.

Marlon hadn't laughed or congratulated him. Bewildered,
frightened by the daring of it and the incomprehensibility,
he fumbled to light a fresh cigarette, another of the sixty he
would smoke that day. Cigarettes were all he had, a tenuous
hold on that real world in which his mother, sixteen years
before, had named him after a famous actor. The smoke
flowed from his loose lips. In a way, but for that cigarette,
he might have been an actor in a miracle play perhaps or in a
chorus of madmen. On that day as on all the others that followed, he walked behind them as they made their way back
through the shaded aisles, under the leather-leaved ilexes,
between the little houses of the dead.

In the hut there was tea to be drunk, and then home, the
foreman off to his semidetached and his comfortable wife,
Marlon to his mother and stuffy room and television com-
mercials, John to his bedsit, Gilly (as John, the favoured,
was now privileged to be told) to the arms of a casino own-
er's wife whose husband lacked a gravedigger's virility.

The chapel was built of yellowish-grey stones. It had an
octagonal nave, and on its floor thin, hair-like grass grew up
between the flags. To one of its sides was attached a square
tower, surmounted at each angle by a thin ornamented spire.
The four spires, weather-worn, corroded, stained, were like
four needles encrusted with rust. The workmen used the
chapel as a repository for pieces of broken stone and iron
rails. Even Gilly's bullying could not make Marlon go inside. He was afraid of Gilly and the foreman, but not so
afraid as he was of the echoing chapel and of the dust be-
neath his feet.

Gilly said, 'What'd you do, Marl, if you turned round
now and it wasn't me here but a skeleton in a shroud, Marl?'

'Leave him alone,' said John, and when they were alone
in the nave, 'You know he's a bit retarded.'

'Big words you use, John. I call him cracked. D'you

know what he said to me yesterday? All them graves are
going to open up and the dead bodies come out. On some
special day that's going to be. What day's that then? I said.
But he only wobbled his head.'

'The dreadful Day of Judgement,' said John, 'when the
secrets of all hearts shall be revealed.'

'Wouldn't suit me, that. Some of them old skulls'd blush
a bit if I told them what I'd been getting up to last night. The
secrets of all hearts? Open some of them up and I'd have a
good many blokes on my track, not to mention that old
git, you-know-who. Break his bloody roulette wheel, he
would.'

'Over your head, no doubt,' said John.

'A short life and a randy one, that's what I say.' They
came out into the cold, pale sunlight. 'Here, have a shufty at
this. Angelina Clara Bowyer, 1816 to 1839. Same age as
what you are, mate, and she'd had five kids! Must have
worn her old man out.'

'It wore her out,' said John, and he seemed to see her with
her piled plaited hair and her long straight dress and the consumption in her face. He saw the young husband mourning
among those five bread-and-butter-fed children, the crepe
on his hat, the black coat. Under a sky like this, the sun a
white puddle in layered cloud, he came with the clergyman
and the mourners and the coffin-bearers to lay her in the
earth. The flowers withered in the biting wind — or did they
bring flowers to funerals then? He didn't know, and not
knowing broke the vision and brought him back to the clink
of spade against granite, the smell of Marlon's cigarette,
Gilly talking, talking, as boringly as an old woman of her
aches and pains only he was talking of sex.

They always stopped work at four now the dusk came
early. 'Nights are drawing in,' said the foreman, brewing
tea, filling up with dog ends the can Gilly had found in the
grave.

'When'll we get it over with?' Marlon faltered, coming close to the stove, coughing a little.

'Depends on what we've got to get over,' said the foreman. 'Digging a bit here, clearing a bit there. My guess is that council fellow'll come round one of these days and say, That's it, lads, now you can leave it to the squirrels.'

Gilly was looking at his calendar, turning over the November nightdress girl to the December Santa Claus girl. 'If I had my way they'd level it all over, the centre bit, and put grass down, make the whole place a park. That's healthy, that is. Somewhere a young kid could take his girl. Lover's Lane Park, that'd be a good name. I'd like to see real birds there, not them bloody crows.'

'You can't do that,' said Marlon. 'There's the dead people in there.'

'So what? There was dead people round the edges, but they took them up. They done something — what they call it, John?'

'They deconsecrated the ground.'

'Hear what John says? He's educated, he knows.'

Marlon got up, the cigarette clinging to his lip. 'You mean they dug them up? There was others and they dug them up?'

' 'Course they did. You didn't think they was under there, did you?'

'Then where'll they be when the Day comes? How'll they lift up the stones and come out?'

'Here, for Christ's sake,' said the foreman, 'that's enough of that, young Marlon. I don't reckon your mum'd better take you to church no more if that's what you come out with.'

'They must come out, they must come and judge,' Marlon cried, and then the foreman told him sharply to shut up, for even he could be shaken by this sort of thing, with the darkness crowding in on the hut, and the heart of the cemetery a black mound horned by the spires of the chapel.

John wondered what church Marlon went to, that of some strange sect perhaps. Or was it only his incomplete brain that distorted the accepted meaning of the Day of Judgement into this version of his own? The resentful dead, the judging dead, lying censorious in the earth.

For his part, he had at first seen the cemetery as no more than a wooded knoll and the stones no more than granite outcroppings. It was not so now. The names in inscriptions, studied by him quietly or derisively read out by Gilly, evoked images of their bearers. James Calhoun Stokes, 1798–1862, Merchant of this City; 'Upright in all his dealings, he stood firm to meet his Maker'. Gilly had an obscene rendering of that, of course. Thomas Charles Macpherson, 1802–79, Master Builder; 'Blest are the Pure in Heart'. Lucy Matilda Osborne, 1823–96; 'Her submissive duty to her husband and devotion to her sons was exceeded only by her pious adoration of her God'. John saw them in cutaway coats, in bombazine gowns, or night-capped on their deathbeds.

But Marlon saw them as a magisterial procession. Listening, watching, waiting perhaps for the ultimate outrage.

'What a load of old cobblers! You'll be down there yourself soon, all the fags you get through in a day.' Gilly sat on a toppled stone, laughing. He had been telling John more about the casino man's wife, trying to find among the statues they had piled up one whose figure might be comparable to hers. Britannias, muses, embodiments of virtues or arts, they lay prostrate, their blank grey or bronze faces all staring upwards at the clouded sky.

'What are we going to do with them?' Marlon said in the voice that was as desperate when he asked about trivialities as when he gave his prophet-like cries.

'Ask the foreman,' said John.

'He won't bloody know.' And Gilly lifted on to his lap the bronze that was nearly nude, just veiled over her loins with metal drapery. 'Randy old devil, he must have been,

that Sidney George Whatsit, having her sitting on top of him
when he was dead.'

'He was a historian, the plaque says,' said John. 'She's
supposed to be Clio, the Muse of History. That's why she's
got a scroll in her hand.' And then, because he was bored
with Gilly and afraid for Marlon, 'Let's stick them all in the
chapel till the council guy comes.'

But Gilly refused to abandon the huge joke of caressing
the bronze. Every reachable inch of her anatomy was examined until, suddenly, he jumped up, leaving her to roll into
one of the muddy ruts the truck had made, and ran up to the
pillared monument from whose dome she had toppled. He
stood inside, a satyr, John thought, in a temple defiled by
northern rains. He threw up his arms.

'I said you was a randy old goat, Sidney, and so you was!
I had a bird called Clio once myself, real hot stuff.' His
shouts punctured the thick greyness, the silence, the fog-
textured air. He leapt down the steps, kicking a gravestone
here, a marble urn there, and perched on a broken column.
'Come out, all the lot of you, if you want, only you can't because you're bloody dead!'

And then Marlon made a horrible sound, the moan a man
makes in sleep, in a nightmare, when he thinks he is screaming. He got into the cab of the truck and hunched there.

'You stupid bastard.' John picked up Marlon's fallen cigarette packet, brushed the grit off it. 'D'you have to act like
a kid of ten?'

'Got to get some sort of kick out of this dump,' Gilly said
sulkily. 'Dead-end hole.'

'Well, that's what it is, isn't it? What d'you expect? A
bar? Booze? Bring on the dancing girls?'

Gilly started to laugh again, picked up his muse again. 'I
wouldn't mind this dancing girl. Don't reckon they'd miss
her, do you? She'd look O.K. in my place. I could stand her
on the table.'

'What for?'

'People have statues, don't they? They've got them in the town hall. It'd give my place a bit of class.'

'Come on,' said John, 'let's stick the lot of them in the chapel. The foreman'll do his nut if he sees you going off with that. She's too big to go under your jacket.'

So they piled the statues and the urns in the chapel, and Gilly amused himself by shouting insults and obscenities which the lofty walls echoed back at him, black pigeons, white doves flapping from the crannies in fear.

'What d'you do in that room of yours, John? Must be a real drag all on your own night after night. Fancy coming over to my bird's place? She's got a real dishy friend. We could have ourselves a ball, and I don't mean wining and dining.'

No, thanks, John said, and softened his refusal by saying he had to study which impressed Gilly. It wasn't that he was a prude so much as that the idea of association with Gilly's friends offended some snobbish delicacy in his nature, some fastidiousness. Better the speechless company of James Calhoun Stokes and Angelina Bowyer and the historian, better, in the evenings, the dreams of them and the wonderings about their lost lives. Though, in refusing, he thought it likely that brash insensitive Gilly might not take his no for an answer but turn up one night with his girl and that other girl to rout him out. He feared it a little, but not with Marlon's obsessional dread of threats from another world.

When at last Gilly did come, it was on a cold moonlit night, and he came alone.

'I'm going to split,' said Gilly, 'I'm getting the hell out. All good things come to an end. You can tell the foreman in the morning, O.K.? I'm going south. I've got a girl in London, worships the ground I tread on, poor cow. She'll take me in. But that's between you and I, right?'

'But why?'

'He's found out, her old man, and I reckon he'll have his heavies out gunning for me. He's beat her up — bunch of bloody gangsters that lot are. I'll miss her.' The tears stood in his eyes, and John stared, amazed, confounded. 'Poor cow,' said Gilly, the epithet an endearment, a caress.

'D'you want me to come to the station with you?'

'No need for that. I only come in to tell you to tell the foreman. Anyway, I got something to do first, get that statue, that Clio. The train don't go till eleven, and I want her.' He turned half away. 'For a souvenir like, she's the dead spitting image.'

'You'd go into the cemetery tonight, for *that*?'

'Like I said, I want her.' His eyes, glazed, held a pathetic hunger. Of love, in those bare words, he had expressed all he knew how to. On lechery only he was articulate. 'It's moonlight,' he said. 'I've got a torch. I'll climb the wall.'

'Goodbye, Gilly,' said John. 'Good luck.'

In the morning the sky was coppery, grey above, reddish on the horizon where the sun hung. The Winter Solstice had come.

'It's like the end of the world,' said Marlon.

The foreman came in, rubbing his hands. 'Going to have snow before the day's over. Gilly's late.' John told him Gilly wasn't coming in. He didn't tell him why not, and he expected an outburst. But the foreman only stuck out his lip and put the kettle on and helped himself to one of Marlon's cigarettes.

'No loss, that,' he said. 'We shan't miss him. And if I'm not much mistaken we'll all be laid off by tonight when this dump's snowed up. You'll be able to get yourselves dug in nice for Christmas, lads.'

Marlon showed no inclination to leave the stuffy warmth of the hut, where the foreman now had a brazier of coke, for the raw air and yellowed dimness of the cemetery. But the foreman wanted to be rid of them, to be on his own, to be idle and warm in peace. He took down Gilly's calendar and pushed it among the glowing coke, and the last John saw of it was the glossy tanned body of a naked girl gyrating in the fire. They moved out into the chill of the shortest day, the foreman hurrying them along by cleaning frost off the truck's windscreen himself.

John expected trouble from the boy, so forbidding was the cemetery in the gloom and under that strange sky. But Marlon, when John had repeated several times that Gilly was not coming, when this had at last sunk in, became more cheerful and more like a normal person than John had ever seen him. He even laughed. He pushed John about in the cab, and when this made the truck swerve, he hooted with laughter.

But when they had come to the centre and were working on clearing the main aisle, he fell silent, though he seemed tranquil enough. All those months John had longed for peace, for a respite from Gilly's ceaseless bragging and innuendo, but now he had it he felt only uneasy. Being alone up here with Marlon had something to do with it. He despised himself for being afraid of a poor retarded boy, yet he was afraid. The thickening atmosphere was part of it, and the windless cold, and the increasing darkness like an eclipse, and the way Marlon would stand for whole minutes on end, staring vacantly, swinging his spade. But what made him long for the snow to begin and drive them back to the hut was Marlon's new habit, now Gilly was not here to deride him, of touching the gravestones and seeming to whisper to them. That he did this reverently and cautiously did nothing to ease John's mind. It was as if he were placating the dead, assuring them that now all would be well. And John had an awareness, growing in intensity as the time slowly passed, that the cemetery had somehow undergone a change. For him it had been just a place to work in, later an abode of sadness and the lost past, never till now macabre. Perhaps much of this feeling was due to the strangeness of the day itself, the permanent twilight, the

knowledge that in these hours the earth had turned to its ultimate distance away from the sun.

Yet it was more than that. That might account for the dis-
tortions he seemed to see, so that the tombs appeared more
closely crowded and the chapel tower taller and darker, but
not for his sensation that there had taken place in the cemetery since he had last seen it, some upheaval and some outrage. It was when these fancies grew so strong as to make
him imagine some actual physical change, the positions of
the slabs and stones altered, that he looked at his watch and
told Marlon they could stop now for their midday meal.

The foreman said to bring down one truck-load of rubble
from the chapel, and then they could knock off. The sky had
lightened a little, becoming uniformly livid, but still they
needed the headlights on. The pale misty shafts of light
probed the undergrowth and died into blackness. They
parked beside the tower.

'Can you make an effort and come in?' said John, 'Or do I
have to do it on my own?'

Marlon managed a sheepish, crafty smile. 'You go first.'

The rubble was heaped against the furthest side of the oc-
tagon. He saw Gilly before he got there. Gilly was lying on
his back among the muses and the virgins, his head, his
face, a mass of black clotted blood to which fragments and
crumbs of stone adhered. Clio, memento of love, had rolled
from his grasp. His eyes still stared, as if they still saw those
meters-out of vengeance.

'Gilly, Gilly!' John cried, and the eight walls called back,
'Gilly, Gilly!' — calling them to Marlon as he came through
the tower and into the nave.

Marlon did not speak Gilly's name. He gave a great cry.

'The dead people came out! The dead people judged him!
The day has come, the end of the world . . . the Day, the
Day, the Day!'

From the eaves, out of the broken roof, the birds came,
circling, cawing, a great rush of wings. And the echo roared

like a knell. John stumbled out after Marlon, after the flying figure that cried like a prophet in the wilderness, into a whiteness that cleaned the world.

In great shaggy flakes, the snow had begun to fall.

A Glowing
Future

'Six should be enough,' he said. 'We'll say six tea chests, then, and one trunk. If you'll deliver them tomorrow, I'll get the stuff all packed and maybe your people could pick them up Wednesday.' He made a note on a bit of paper. 'Fine,' he said. 'Round about lunchtime tomorrow.'

She hadn't moved. She was still sitting in the big oak-armed chair at the far end of the room. He made himself look at her and he managed a kind of grin, pretending all was well.

'No trouble,' he said. 'They're very efficient.'

'I couldn't believe,' she said, 'that you'd really do it. Not until I heard you on the phone. I wouldn't have thought it possible. You'll really pack up all those things and have them sent off to her.'

They were going to have to go over it all again. Of course they were. It wouldn't stop until he'd got the things out and himself out, away from London and her for good. And he wasn't going to argue or make long defensive speeches. He lit a cigarette and waited for her to begin, thinking that the pubs would be opening in an hour's time and he could go out then and get a drink.

'I don't understand why you came here at all,' she said.

He didn't answer. He was still holding the cigarette box, and now he closed its lid, feeling the coolness of the onyx on his fingertips.

She had gone white. 'Just to get your things? Maurice, did you come back just for that?'

'They are my things,' he said evenly.

'You could have sent someone else. Even if you'd written to me and asked me to do it — '

'I never write letters,' he said.

She moved then. She made a little fluttering with her hand in front of her mouth. 'As if I didn't know!' She gasped, and making a great effort she steadied her voice. 'You were in Australia for a year, a whole year, and you never wrote to me once.'

'I phoned.'

'Yes, twice. The first time to say you loved me and missed me and were longing to come back to me and would I wait for you and there wasn't anyone else was there? And the second time, a week ago, to say you'd be here by Saturday and could I — could I put you up. My God, I'd lived with you for two years, we were practically married, and then you phone and ask if I could put you up!'

'Words,' he said. 'How would you have put it?'

'For one thing, I'd have mentioned Patricia. Oh, yes, I'd have mentioned her. I'd have had the decency, the common humanity, for that. D'you know what I thought when you said you were coming? I ought to know by now how peculiar he is, I thought, how detached, not writing or phoning or anything. But that's Maurice, that's the man I love, and he's coming back to me and we'll get married and I'm so happy!'

'I did tell you about Patricia.'

'Not until after you'd made love to me first.'

He winced. It had been a mistake, that. Of course he hadn't meant to touch her beyond the requisite greeting kiss. But she was very attractive and he was used to her and she seemed to expect it — and oh, what the hell. Women never could understand about men and sex. And there was only one bed, wasn't there? A hell of a scene there'd have been that first night if he'd suggested sleeping on the sofa in here.

'You made love to me,' she said. 'You were so passionate, it was just like it used to be, and then the next morning you told me. You'd got a resident's permit to stay in Australia, you'd got a job all fixed up, you'd met a girl you wanted to marry. Just like that you told me, over breakfast. Have you ever been smashed in the face, Maurice? Have you ever had your dreams trodden on?'

'Would you rather I'd waited longer? As for being smashed in the face — ' he rubbed his cheekbone ' — that's quite a punch you pack.'

She shuddered. She got up and began slowly and stiffly to pace the room. 'I hardly touched you. I wish I'd killed you!' By a small table she stopped. There was a china figurine on it, a bronze paperknife, an onyx pen jar that matched the ashtray. 'All those things,' she said. 'I looked after them for you. I treasured them. And now you're going to have them all shipped out to her. The things we lived with. I used to look at them and think, Maurice bought that when we went to — oh God, I can't believe it. Sent to her!'

He nodded, staring at her. 'You can keep the big stuff,' he said. 'You're specially welcome to the sofa. I've tried sleeping on it for two nights and I never want to see the bloody thing again.'

She picked up the china figurine and hurled it at him. It didn't hit him because he ducked and let it smash against the wall, just missing a framed drawing. 'Mind the Lowry,' he said laconically, 'I paid a lot of money for that.'

She flung herself onto the sofa and burst into sobs. She thrashed about, hammering the cushions with her fists. He wasn't going to be moved by that — he wasn't going to be moved at all. Once he'd packed those things, he'd be off to spend the next three months touring Europe. A free man, free for the sights and the fun and the girls, for a last fling of wild oats. After that, back to Patricia and a home and a job and responsibility. It was a glowing future which this hysterical woman wasn't going to mess up.

'Shut up, Betsy, for God's sake,' he said. He shook her roughly by the shoulder, and then he went out because it was now eleven and he could get a drink.

Betsy made herself some coffee and washed her swollen eyes. She walked about, looking at the ornaments and the books, the glasses and vases and lamps, which he would take from her tomorrow. It wasn't that she much minded losing them, the things themselves, but the barrenness which would be left, and the knowing that they would all be Patricia's.

In the night she had got up, found his wallet, taken out the photographs of Patricia, and torn them up. But she remembered the face, pretty and hard and greedy, and she thought of those bright eyes widening as Patricia unpacked the tea chests, the predatory hands scrabbling for more treasures in the trunk. Doing it all perhaps before Maurice himself got there, arranging the lamps and the glasses and the ornaments in their home for his delight when at last he came.

He would marry her, of course. I suppose she thinks he's faithful to her, Betsy thought, the way I once thought he was faithful to me. I know better now. Poor stupid fool, she doesn't know what he did the first moment he was alone with her, or what he would do in France and Italy. That would be a nice wedding present to give her, wouldn't it, along with all the pretty bric-a-brac in the trunk?

Well, why not? Why not rock their marriage before it had even begun? A letter. A letter to be concealed in, say, that blue-and-white ginger jar. She sat down to write. Dear Patricia — what a stupid way to begin, the way you had to begin a letter even to your enemy.

Dear Patricia: I don't know what Maurice has told you about me, but we have been living here as lovers ever since he arrived. To be more explicit, I mean we have made love, have slept together. Maurice is incapable of being faithful to anyone. If you don't believe me, ask yourself why, if he didn't want me, he didn't stay in a hotel. That's all. Yours — and she signed her name and felt a little better, well enough and steady enough to take a bath and get herself some lunch.

Six tea chests and a trunk arrived on the following day. The chests smelled of tea and had drifts of tea leaves lying in the bottom of them. The trunk was made of silver-coloured metal and had clasps of gold-coloured metal. It was rather a beautiful object, five feet long, three feet high, two feet wide, and the lid fitted so securely it seemed a hermetic sealing.

Maurice began to pack at two o'clock. He used tissue paper and newspapers. He filled the tea chests with kitchen equipment and cups and plates and cutlery, with books, with those clothes of his he had left behind him a year before. Studiously, and with a certain grim pleasure, he avoided everything Betsy might have insisted was hers — the poor cheap things, the stainless steel spoons and forks, the Woolworth pottery, the awful coloured sheets, red and orange and olive, that he had always loathed. He and Patricia would sleep in white linen.

Betsy didn't help him. She watched, chain-smoking. He nailed the lids on the chests and on each lid he wrote in white paint his address in Australia. But he didn't paint in the letters of his own name. He painted Patricia's. This wasn't done to needle Betsy but he was glad to see it was needling her.

He hadn't come back to the flat till one that morning, and of course he didn't have a key. Betsy had refused to let him in, had left him down there in the street, and he had to sit in the car he'd hired till seven. She looked as if she hadn't slept either. Miss Patricia Gordon, he wrote, painting fast and skilfully.

'Don't forget your ginger jar.' said Betsy. 'I don't want it.'

'That's for the trunk.' Miss Patricia Gordon, 23 Burwood Park Avenue, Kew, Victoria, Australia 3101. 'All the pretty things are going in the trunk. I intend it as a special present for Patricia.'

The Lowry came down and was carefully padded and wrapped. He wrapped the onyx ashtray and the pen jar, the alabaster bowl, the bronze paperknife, the tiny Chinese cups, the tall hock glasses. The china figurine, alas . . . he opened the lid of the trunk.

'I hope the customs open it!' Betsy shouted at him. 'I hope they confiscate things and break things! I'll pray every night for it to go to the bottom of the sea before it gets there!'

'The sea,' he said, 'is a risk I must take. As for the customs — ' He smiled. 'Patricia works for them, she's a customs officer — didn't I tell you? I very much doubt if they'll even glance inside.' He wrote a label and pasted it on the side of the trunk. Miss Patricia Gordon, 23 Burwood Park Avenue, Kew. . . 'And now I'll have to go out and get a padlock. Keys, please. If you try to keep me out this time, I'll call the police. I'm still the legal tenant of this flat remember.'

She gave him the keys. When he had gone she put her letter in the ginger jar. She hoped he would close the trunk at once, but he didn't. He left it open, the lid thrown back, the new padlock dangling from the gold-coloured clasp.

'Is there anything to eat?' he said.

'Go and find your own bloody food! Go and find some other woman to feed you!'

He liked her to be angry and fierce; it was her love he feared. He came back at midnight to find the flat in darkness, and he lay down on the sofa with the tea chests standing about him like defenses, like barricades, the white paint showing faintly in the dark. Miss Patricia Gordon. . .

Presently Betsy came in. She didn't put on the light. She

wound her way between the chests, carrying a candle in a saucer which she set down on the trunk. In the candlelight, wearing a long white nightgown, she looked like a ghost, like some wandering madwoman, a Mrs. Rochester, a Woman in White.

'Maurice.'

'Go away, Betsy, I'm tired.'

'Maurice, please. I'm sorry I said all those things. I'm sorry I locked you out.'

'O.K., I'm sorry too. It's a mess, and maybe I shouldn't have done it the way I did. But the best way is for me just to go and my things to go and make a clean split. Right? And now will you please be a good girl and go away and let me get some sleep?'

What happened next he hadn't bargained for. It hadn't crossed his mind. Men don't understand about women and sex. She threw herself on him, clumsily, hungrily. She pulled his shirt open and began kissing his neck and his chest, holding his head, crushing her mouth to his mouth, lying on top of him and gripping his legs with her knees.

He gave her a savage push. He kicked her away, and she fell and struck her head on the side of the trunk. The candle fell off, flared and died in a pool of wax. In the darkness he cursed floridly. He put on the light and she got up, holding her head where there was a little blood.

'Oh, get out, for God's sake,' he said, and he manhandled her out, slamming the door after her.

In the morning, when she came into the room, a blue bruise on her forehead, he was asleep, fully clothed, spread-eagled on his back. She shuddered at the sight of him. She began to get breakfast but she couldn't eat anything. The coffee made her gag and a great nauseous shiver went through her. When she went back to him he was sitting up on the sofa, looking at his plane ticket to Paris.

'The men are coming for the stuff at ten,' he said as if

nothing had happened, 'and they'd better not be late. I have to be at the airport at noon.'

She shrugged. She had been to the depths and she thought he couldn't hurt her any more.

'You'd better close the trunk,' she said absent-mindedly.

'All in good time.' His eyes gleamed. 'I've got a letter to put in yet.'

Her head bowed, the place where it was bruised sore and swollen, she looked loweringly at him. 'You never write letters.'

'Just a note. One can't send a present without a note to accompany it, can one?'

He pulled the ginger jar out of the trunk, screwed up her letter without even glancing at it, and threw it on the floor. Rapidly yet ostentatiously and making sure that Betsy could see, he scrawled across a sheet of paper: *All this is for you, darling Patricia, for ever and ever.*

'How I hate you,' she said.

'You could have fooled me.' He took a large angle lamp out of the trunk and set it on the floor. He slipped the note into the ginger jar, rewrapped it, tucked the jar in between the towels and cushions which padded the fragile objects. 'Hatred isn't the word I'd use to describe the way you came after me last night.'

She made no answer. Perhaps he should have put a heavy object like that lamp in one of the chests, perhaps he should open up one of the chests now. He turned round for the lamp. It wasn't there. She was holding it in both hands.

'I want that, please.'

'Have you ever been smashed in the face, Maurice?' she said breathlessly, and she raised the lamp and struck him with it full on the forehead. He staggered and she struck him again, and again and again, raining blows on his face and on his head. He screamed. He sagged, covering his face with bloody hands. Then with all her strength she gave him a great swinging blow and he fell to his knees, rolled over and at last was stilled and silenced.

There was quite a lot of blood, though it quickly stopped flowing. She stood there looking at him and she was sobbing. Had she been sobbing all the time? She was covered with blood. She tore off her clothes and dropped them in a heap around her. For a moment she knelt beside him, naked and weeping, rocking backwards and forwards, speaking his name, biting her fingers that were sticky with his blood.

But self-preservation is the primal instinct, more powerful than love or sorrow, hatred or regret. The time was nine o'clock, and in an hour those men would come. Betsy fetched water in a bucket, detergent, cloths and a sponge. The hard work, the great cleansing, stopped her tears, quieted her heart and dulled her thoughts. She thought of nothing, working frenziedly, her mind a blank.

When bucket after bucket of reddish water had been poured down the sink and the carpet was soaked but clean, the lamp washed and dried and polished, she threw her clothes into the basket in the bathroom and had a bath. She dressed carefully and brushed her hair. Eight minutes to ten. Everything was clean and she had opened the window, but the dead thing still lay there on a pile of reddened newspapers.

'I loved him,' she said aloud, and she clenched her fists. 'I hated him.'

The men were punctual. They came at ten sharp. They carried the six tea chests and the silver-coloured trunk with the gold-coloured clasps downstairs.

When they had gone and their van had driven away, Betsy sat down on the sofa. She looked at the angle lamp, the onyx pen jar and ashtray, the ginger jar, the alabaster bowls, the hock glasses, the bronze paperknife, the little Chinese cups, and the Lowry that was back on the wall. She was quite calm now and she didn't really need the brandy she had poured for herself.

Of the past she thought not at all and the present seemed to exist only as a palpable nothingness, a thick silence that lay around her. She thought of the future, of three months hence, and into the silence she let forth a steady, rather toneless peal of laughter. Miss Patricia Gordon, 23 Burwood Park Avenue, Kew, Victoria, Australia 3101. The pretty, greedy, hard face, the hands so eager to undo that padlock and prise open those golden clasps to find the treasure within. . .

And how interesting that treasure would be in three months' time, like nothing Miss Patricia Gordon had seen in all her life! It was as well, so that she would recognize it, that it carried on top of it a note in a familiar hand: *All this is for you, darling Patricia, for ever and ever.*

An Outside
Interest

Frightening people used to be a hobby of mine. Perhaps I should rather say an obsession and not people but, specifically, women. Making others afraid *is* enjoyable as everyone discovers who has tried it and succeeded. I suppose it has something to do with power. Most people never really try it so they don't know, but look at the ones who do. Judges, policemen, prison warders, customs officers, tax inspectors. They have a great time, don't they? You don't find them giving up or adopting other methods. Frightening people goes to their heads, they're drunk on it, they live by it. So did I. While other men might go down to the pub with the boys or to football, I went off to Epping Forest and frightened women. It was what you might call my outside interest.

Don't get me wrong. There was nothing — well, nasty, about what I did. You know what I mean by that, I'm sure I don't have to go into details. I'm far from being some sort of pervert, I can tell you. In fact, I err rather on the side of too much moral strictness. Nor am I one of those lonely, deprived men. I'm six feet tall, not bad-looking and, I assure you, entirely physically and mentally normal.

Of course I've tried to analyse myself and discover my motives. Was my hobby ever any more than an antidote to boredom? By anyone's standards the life I lead would be classed as pretty dull, selling tickets and answering passengers' queries at Anglo-Mercian Airways terminal, living in a semi in Muswell Hill, going to tea with my mother-in-law on Sundays and having an annual fortnight in a holiday flat in South Devon. I got married very young. Adventure wasn't exactly a conspicuous feature of my existence. The biggest thing that happened to me was when we thought one of our charters had been hijacked in Greece, and that turned out to be a false alarm.

My wife is a nervous sort of girl. Mind you, she has cause to be, living where we do close to Highgate Wood and Queens Wood. A woman takes her life in her hands, walking alone in those places. Carol used to regale me with stories — well, she still does.

'At twenty past five in the afternoon! It was still broad daylight. He raped her and cut her in the face, she had to have seventeen stitches in her face and neck.'

She doesn't drive and if she comes home from anywhere after dark I always go down to the bus stop to meet her. She won't even walk along the Muswell Hill Road because of the woods on either side.

'If you see a man on his own in a place like that you naturally ask yourself what he's doing there, don't you? A young man, just walking aimlessly about. It's not as if he had a dog with him. It makes your whole body go tense and you get a sort of awful crawling sensation all over you. If you didn't come and meet me I don't think I'd go out at all.'

Was it that which gave me the idea? At any rate it made me think about women and fear. Things are quite different for a man, he never thinks about being afraid of being in dark or lonely places. I'm sure I never have and therefore, until I got all this from Carol, I never considered how important this business of being scared when out alone might be to them. When I came to understand it gave me a funny feeling of excitement.

And then I actually frightened a woman myself — by chance. My usual way of going to work is to cut through Queens Wood to Highgate tube station and take the Northern Line down into London. When the weather is very bad I go to the station by bus but most of the time I walk there and back and the way through the wood is a considerable short cut. I was coming back through the wood at about six one evening in March. It was dusk, growing dark. The lamps, each a good distance apart from each other, which light the paths, were lit, but I often think these give the place a rather more bleak and sinister appearance than if it were quite dark. You leave a light behind you and walk along a dim shadowy avenue towards the next lamp which gleams faintly some hundred yards ahead. And no sooner is it reached, an acid yellow glow among the bare branches, than you leave it behind again to negotiate the next dark stretch. I thought about how it must be to be a woman walking through the wood and, yes, I gloried in my maleness and my freedom from fear.

Then I saw the girl coming. She was walking along the path from Priory Gardens. It came into my head that she would be less wary of me if I continued as I had been, marching briskly and purposefully towards Wood Vale, swinging along and looking like a man homeward bound to his family and his dinner. There was no definite intent present in my mind when I slackened my pace, then stopped and stood still. But as soon as I'd done that I knew I was going to carry it through. The girl came up to where the paths converged and where the next lamp was. She gave me a quick darting look. I stood there in a very relaxed way and I returned her look with a blank stare. I suppose I consciously, out of some sort of devilment, made my eyes fixed and glazed and let my mouth go loose. Anyway, she turned very quickly away and began to walk much faster.

She had high heels so she couldn't go very fast, not as fast as I could, just strolling along behind her. I gained on her until I was a yard behind.

I could smell her fear. She was wearing a lot of perfume and

her sweat seemed to potentiate it so that there came to me a
whiff and then a wave of heady, mixed-up animal and floral
scent. I breathed it in, I breathed heavily. She began to run and
I strode after her. What she did then was unexpected. She
stopped, turned round and cried out in a tremulous terrified
voice: 'What do you want?'

I stopped too and gave her the same look. She held her handbag out to me. 'Take it!'

The joke had gone far enough. I lived round there anyway, I
had my wife and son to think of. I put on a cockney voice.
'Keep your bag, love. You've got me wrong.'

And then, to reassure her, I turned back along the path and
let her escape to Wood Vale and the lights and the start of the
houses. But I can't describe what a feeling of power and
— well, triumphant manhood and what's called machismo the
encounter gave me. I felt grand. I swaggered into my house and
Carol said had I had a Premium Bond come up?

Since I'm being strictly truthful in this account, I'd better
add the other consequence of what happened in the wood, even
though it does rather go against the grain with me to mention
things like that. I made love to Carol that night and it was a lot
better than it had been for a long time, in fact it was sensational
for both of us. And I couldn't kid myself that it was due to anything but my adventure with the girl.

Next day I looked at myself in the mirror with all the lights
off but the little tubular one over our bed, and I put on the same
look I'd given the girl when she turned in my direction under
the lamp. I can tell you I nearly frightened myself. I've said I'm
not bad looking and that's true but I'm naturally pale and since
I'm thin, my face tends to be a bit gaunt. In the dim light my
eyes seemed sunk in deep sockets and my mouth hung loose in
a vacant mindless way. I stepped back from the glass so that I
could see the whole of myself, slouching, staring, my arms
hanging. There was no doubt I had the potential of being a
woman-frightener of no mean calibre.

They say it's the first step that counts. I had taken the first

step but the second was bigger and it was weeks before I took
it. I kept telling myself not to be a fool, to forget those mad
ideas. Besides, surely I could see I'd soon be in trouble if I
made a habit of frightening women in Queens Wood, on my
own doorstep. But I couldn't stop thinking about it. I remembered how wonderful I'd felt that evening, how tall I'd walked
and what a man I'd been.

The funny thing was what a lot of humiliating things seemed
to happen to me at that time, between the Queens Wood inci-
dent and the next occasion. A woman at the air terminal actually spat at me. I'm not exaggerating. Of course she was drunk,
smashed out of her mind on duty-free Scotch, but she spat at
me and I had to stand there in the middle of the ticket hall with
all those tourists milling about, and wipe the spittle off my uniform. Then I got a reprimand for being discourteous to a passenger. It was totally unjust and, strictly speaking, I should
have resigned on the spot, only I've got a wife and son and jobs
aren't easy to come by at present. There was all that and trouble
at home as well with Carol nagging me to take her on holiday
with this girl friend of hers and her husband to Minorca instead
of our usual Salcombe fortnight. I told her straight we couldn't
afford it but I didn't like being asked in return why I couldn't
earn as much as Sheila's Mike.

My manhood was at a low ebb. Then Sheila and Mike asked
us to spend the day with them, Carol, Timothy and me. They
had been neighbours of ours but had just moved away to a new
house in one of those outer suburbs that are really in Essex. So I
drove the three of us out to Theydon Bois and made my ac-
quaintance with Epping Forest.

There are sixty-four square miles of forest, lying on the
northeastern borders of London. But when you drive from the
Wake Arms to Theydon along a narrow road bordered by
woodland, stretches of turf and undergrowth, little coppices of
birch trees, you can easily believe yourself in the depths of the
country. It seems impossible that London is only fourteen or
fifteen miles away. The forest is green and silent and from a car

looks unspoilt, though of course it can't be. We passed a
woman walking a very unguard-like dog, a tiny Maltese terrier . . . That gave me the idea. Why shouldn't I come out here?
Why shouldn't I try my frightening act out here where no one
knew me?

Two days after that I did. It was spring and the evenings
stayed light till nearly eight. I didn't take the car. Somehow it
didn't seem to me as if the sort of person I was going to be,
going to *act*, would have a car. The journey was awful, enough
to deter anyone less determined than I. I went straight from
work, taking the Central Line tube as far as Loughton and then
a bus up the hills and into the forest. At the Wake Arms I got
off and began to walk down the hill, not on the pavement but a
few yards inside the forest itself. I didn't see a woman on her
own until I had reached the houses of Theydon and begun the
return trip. I had gone about a hundred yards up again when she
came out of one of the last houses, a young girl in jeans and a
jacket, her hands in her pockets.

It was clear she was going to walk to the Wake Arms. Or so
I thought. For a while I walked, keeping step with her, but unseen among the hawthorn and crab apple bushes, the tangle of
brambles. I let us get a quarter of a mile away from the houses
before I showed myself and then I stepped out on to the pavement ahead of her. I turned round to face her and stood there,
staring in the way I'd practised in the mirror.

She wasn't nervous. She was brave. It was only very briefly
that she hesitated. But she didn't quite dare walk past me. Instead she crossed the road. There's never much traffic on that
road and so far not a single car had passed. She crossed the
road, walking faster. I crossed too but behind her and I walked
along behind her. Presently she began to run, so of course I ran
too, though not fast enough to catch her up, just enough to gain
on her a little.

We had been going on like that for some minutes, the Wake
Arms still a mile off, when she suddenly doubled back, hared
across the road and began running back the way she had come.

That finished me for chasing her. I stood there and laughed. I laughed long and loud, I felt so happy and free, I felt so much all-conquering power that I — I alone, humble, ordinary, dull *me* — could inspire such fear.

After that I took to going to Epping Forest as a regular thing. Roughly speaking, I'd say it would have been once a fortnight. Since I do shift work, four till midnight just as often as ten till six, I sometimes managed to go in the daytime. A lot of women are alone at home in the daytime and have no men to escort them when they go out. I never let it go more than two weeks without my going there and occasionally I'd go more often, if I was feeling low in spirits, for instance, or Carol and I had a row or I got depressed over money. It did me so much good, I wish I could make you understand how much. Just think what it is you do that gives you a tremendous lift, driving a car really fast or going disco dancing or getting high on something — well, frightening women did all that for me and then some. After-wards it was like Christmas, it was almost like being in love.

And there was no harm in it, was there? I didn't hurt them. There's a French saying: it gives me so much pleasure and you so little pain. That was the way it was for me and them, though it wasn't without pleasure for them either. Imagine how they must have enjoyed talking about it afterwards, going into all the details like Carol did, distorting the facts, exaggerating, mak-ing themselves for a while the centre of attention.

For all I knew they may have got up search parties, hus-bands and boyfriends and fathers all out in a pack looking for me, all having a great time as people invariably do when they're hunting something or someone. After all, when all was said and done, what did I do? Nothing. I didn't molest them or insult them or try to touch them, I merely stood and looked at them and ran after them — or ran when they ran which isn't necessarily the same thing.

There was no harm in it. Or so I thought. I couldn't see what harm there could ever be, and believe me, I thought about this quite a lot, for I'm just as guilt-ridden as the rest of us. I thought about it, justifying myself, keeping guilt at bay. Young women don't have heart attacks and fall down dead because a man chases them. Young women aren't left with emotional traumas because a man stares at them. The oldest woman I ever frightened was the one with the Maltese terrier and she was no more than forty. I saw her again on my third or fourth visit and followed her for a while, stepping out from behind bushes and standing in her path. She used the same words the girl in Queens Wood had used, uttered in the same strangled voice: 'What is it you want?'

I didn't answer her. I had mercy on her and her little ineffectual dog and I melted away into the woodland shades. The next one who asked me that I answered with professorial gravity: 'Merely collecting lichens, madam.'

It was proof enough of how harmless I was that there was never a sign of a policeman in that area. I'm sure none of them told the police, for they had nothing to tell. They had only what they imagined and what the media had led them to expect. Yet harm did come from it, irrevocable harm and suffering and shame.

No doubt by now you think you've guessed. The inevitable must have happened, the encounter which any man who makes a practice of intimidating women is bound to have sooner or later, when the tables are turned on him. Yes, that did happen but it wasn't what stopped me. Being seized by the arm, hurled in the air and laid out, sprawled and bruised, by a judo black belt, was just an occupational hazard. I've always been glad, though, that I behaved like a gentleman. I didn't curse her or shout abuse. I merely got up, rubbed my legs and my elbows, made her a little bow and walked off in the direction of the Wake. Carol wanted to know how I'd managed to get green stains all over my clothes and I think to this day she believes it was from lying on the grass in a park somewhere with another woman. As if I would!

That attack on me deterred me. It didn't put me off. I let three weeks go by, three miserable yearning weeks, and then I

went back to the Wake road one sunny July morning and had
one of my most satisfying experiences. A girl walking, not on
the road, but taking a short cut through the forest itself. I
walked parallel to her, sometimes letting her catch a glimpse of
me. I knew she did, for like it had been with the girl in Queens
Wood, I could sense and smell her fear.

I strolled out from the bushes at last and stood ahead of her,
waiting. She didn't dare approach me, she didn't know what to
do. At length she turned back and I followed her, threading my
way among the bushes until she must have thought I had gone,
then appearing once more on the path ahead. This time she
turned off to the left, running, and I let her go. Laughing the
way I always did, out loud and irrepressibly, I let her go. I
hadn't done her any harm. Think of the relief she must have felt
when she knew she'd got away from me and was safe. Think of
her going home and telling her mother or her sister or her husband all about it.

You could even say I'd done her a good turn. Most likely I'd
warned her off going out in the forest on her own and therefore
protected her from some real pervert or molester of women.

It was a point of view, wasn't it? You could make me out a
public benefactor. I showed them what could happen. I was
like the small electric shock that teaches a child not to play with
the wires. Or that's what I believed. Till I learned that even a
small shock can kill.

I was out in the forest, on the Wake road, when I had a piece
of luck. It was autumn and getting dark at six, the earliest I'd
been able to get there, and I didn't have much hope of any
woman being silly enough to walk down that road alone in the
dark. I had got off the bus at the Wake Arms and was walking
slowly down the hill when I saw this car parked ahead of me at
the kerb. Even from a distance I could hear the horrible noise it
made as the driver tried to start it, that anguished grinding you
get when ignition won't take place.

The offside door opened and a woman got out. She was on
her own. She reached back into the car and turned the lights

off, slammed the door, locked it and began walking down the hill towards Theydon. I had stepped in among the trees and she hadn't yet seen me. I followed her, working out what technique I should use this time. Pursuing her at a run to start with was what I decided on.

I came out on to the pavement about a hundred yards behind her and began running after her, making as much noise with my feet as I could. Of course she stopped and turned round as I knew she would. Probably she thought I was a saviour who was going to do something about her car for her. She looked round, waiting for me, and as soon as I caught her eye I veered off into the forest once more. She gave a sort of shrug, turned and walked on. She wasn't frightened yet.

It was getting dark, though, and there was no moon. I caught her up and walked alongside her, very quietly, only three or four yards away, yet in among the trees of the forest. By then we were out of sight of the parked car and a long way from being in sight of the lights of Theydon. The road was dark, though far from being impenetrably black. I trod on a twig deliberately and made it snap and she turned swiftly and saw me.

She jumped. She looked away immediately and quickened her pace. Of course she didn't have a chance with me, a five-foot woman doesn't with a six-foot man. The fastest she could walk was still only my strolling pace.

There hadn't been a car along the road since I'd been following her. Now one came. I could see its lights welling and dipping a long way off, round the twists in the road. She went to the edge of the pavement and held up her hand the way a hitchhiker does. I stayed where I was to see what would happen. What had I done, after all? Only been there. But the driver didn't stop for her. Of course he didn't, no more than I would have done in his place. We all know the sort of man who stops his car to pick up smartly dressed, pretty hitchhikers at night and we know what he's after.

The next driver didn't stop either. I was a little ahead of her by then, still inside the forest, and in his headlights I saw her face. She *was* pretty, not that that aspect particularly interested me, but I saw that she was pretty and that she belonged to the same type as Carol, a small slender blonde with rather sharp features and curly hair.

The darkness seemed much darker after the car lights had passed. I could tell she was a little less tense now, she probably hadn't seen me for the past five minutes, she might have thought I'd gone. And I was tempted to call it a day, give up after a quarter of an hour, as I usually did when I'd had my fun.

I wish to God I had. I went on with it for the stupidest of reasons. I went on with it because I wanted to go in the same direction as she was going, down into Theydon and catch the tube train from there, rather than go back and hang about waiting for a bus. I could have waited and let her go. I didn't. Out of some sort of perverse need, I kept step with her and then I came out of the forest and got on to the pavement behind her.

I walked along, gaining on her, but quietly. The road dipped, wound a little. I got two or three yards behind her, going very softly, she didn't know I was there, and then I began a soft whistling, a hymn tune it was, the Crimond version of *The Lord is My Shepherd*. What a choice!

She spun round. I thought she was going to say something but I don't think she could. Her voice was strangled by fear.

She turned again and began to run. She could run quite fast, that tiny vulnerable blonde girl.

The car lights loomed up over the road ahead. They were full-beam, undipped headlights, blazing blue-white across the surrounding forest, showing up every tree and making long black shadows spring from their trunks. I jumped aside and crouched down in the long grass. She ran into the road, holding up both arms and crying: 'Help me! Help me!'

He stopped. I had a moment's tension when I thought he might get out and come looking for me, but he didn't. He pushed open the passenger door from inside. The girl got in, they waited, sitting there for maybe half a minute, and then the white Ford Capri moved off.

It was a relief to me to see that car disappear over the top of the hill. And I realized, to coin a very appropriate phrase, that I wasn't yet out of the wood. What could be more likely than that girl and the car driver would either phone or call in at Loughton police station? I knew I'd better get myself down to Theydon as fast as possible.

As it happened I did so without meeting or being passed by another vehicle. I was walking along by the village green when the only cars I saw came along. On the station platform I had to wait for nearly half an hour before a train came, but no policeman came either. I had got away with it again.

In a way. There are worse things than being punished for one's crimes. One of those is not being punished for them. I am suffering for what I did of course by not being allowed — that is, by not allowing myself — to do it again. And I shall never forget that girl's face, so pretty and vulnerable and frightened. It comes to me a lot in dreams.

The first time it appeared to me was in a newspaper photograph, two days after I had frightened her on the Wake road. The newspaper was leading on the story of her death and that was why it used the picture. On the previous morning, when she had been dead twelve hours, her body had been found, stabbed and mutilated, in a field between Epping and Harlow. Police were looking for a man, thought to be the driver of a white Ford Capri.

Her rescuer, her murderer. Then what was I?

A Case of
Coincidence

Of the several obituaries which appeared on the death of Michael Lestrange not one mentioned his connection with the Wrexlade murders. Memories are short, even journalists' memories, and it may be that the newspapermen who wrote so glowingly and so mournfully about him were mere babes in arms, or not even born, at the time. For the murders, of course, took place in the early fifties, before the abolition of capital punishment.

Murder is the last thing one would associate with the late Sir Michael, eminent cardiac specialist, physician to Her Royal Highness the Duchess of Albany, and author of that classic work, the last word on its subject, so succinctly entitled *The Heart*. Sir Michael did not destroy life, he saved it. He was as far removed from Kenneth Edward Brannel, the Wrexlade Strangler, as he was from the carnivorous spider which crept across his consulting room window. Those who knew him well would say that he had an almost neurotic horror of the idea of taking life. Euthanasia he had refused to discuss, and he had opposed with all his vigour the legalizing of abortion.

Until last March when an air crash over the North Atlantic claimed him among its two hundred fatalities, he had been a man one automatically thought of as life-enhancing, as having on countless occasions defied death on behalf of others. Yet he seemed to have had no private life, no family, no circle to move in, no especially beautiful home. He lived for his work. He was not married and few knew he ever had been, still fewer that his wife had been the last of the Wrexlade victims.

There were four others and all five of them died as a result of being strangled by the outsized, bony hands of Kenneth Edward Brannel. Michael Lestrange, by the way, had exceptionally narrow, well-shaped hands, dextrous and precise. Brannel's have been described as resembling bunches of bananas. In her study of the Wrexlade case, the criminologist Miss Georgina Hallam Saul, relates how Brannel, in the condemned cell, talked about committing these crimes to a prison officer. He had never understood why he killed those women, he didn't dislike women or fear them.

'It's like when I was a kid and in a shop and there was no one about,' he is alleged to have said. 'I had to take something, I couldn't help myself. I didn't even do it sort of of my own will. One minute it'd be on the shelf and the next in my pocket. It was the same with those girls. I had to get my hands on their throats. Everything'd go dark and when it cleared my hands'd be round their throats and the life all squeezed out. . .'

He was twenty-eight, an agricultural labourer, illiterate, classified as educationally subnormal. He lived with his widowed father, also a farm worker, in a cottage on the outskirts of Wrexlade in Essex. During 1953 he strangled Wendy Cutforth, Maureen Hunter, Ann Daly and Mary Trenthyde without the police having the least suspicion of his guilt. Approximately a month elapsed between each of these murders, though there was no question of Brannel killing at the full moon or anything of that sort. Four weeks af-

ter Mary Trenthyde's death he was arrested and charged with
murder, for the strangled body of Norah Lestrange had been
discovered in a ditch less than a hundred yards from his cottage. They found him guilty of murder in November of that
same year, twenty-five days later he was executed.

'A terrible example of injustice,' Michael Lestrange used
to say. 'If the M'Naughten Rules apply to anybody they
surely applied to poor Brannel. With him it wasn't only a
matter of not knowing that what he was doing was wrong
but of not knowing he was doing it at all till it was over. We
have hanged a poor idiot who had no more idea of evil than a
stampeding animal has when it tramples on a child.'

People thought it amazingly magnanimous of Michael
that he could talk like this when it was his own wife who had
been murdered. She was only twenty-five and they had been
married less than three years.

It is probably best to draw on Miss Hallam Saul for the
most accurate and comprehensive account of the Wrexlade
stranglings. She attended the trial, every day of it, which
Michael Lestrange did not. When prosecuting counsel, in
his opening speech, came to describe Norah Lestrange's
reasons for being in the neighbourhood of Wrexlade that
night, and to talk of the Dutchman and the hotel at Chelmsford, Michael got up quietly and left the court. Miss Hallam
Saul's eyes, and a good many other pairs of eyes, followed
him with compassion. Nevertheless, she didn't spare his
feelings in her book. Why should she? Like everyone else
who wrote about Brannel and Wrexlade, she was appalled
by the character of Norah Lestrange. This was the fifties, remember, and the public were not used to hearing of young
wives who admitted shamelessly to their husbands that one
man was not enough for them. Michael had been obliged to
state the facts to the police and the facts were that he had
known for months that his wife spent nights in this Chelmsford hotel with Jan Vandepeer, a businessman on his way

from The Hook and Harwich to London. She had told him so quite openly.

'Darling. . .' Taking his arm and leading him to sit close beside her while she fondled his hand. 'Darling, I absolutely have to have Jan, I'm crazy about him. I do have to have other men, I'm made that way. It's nothing to do with the way I feel about you, though, you do see that, don't you?'

These words he didn't, of course, render verbatim. The gist was enough.

'It won't be all that often, Mike darling, once a month at most. Jan can't fix a trip more than once a month. Chelmsford's so convenient for both of us and you'll hardly notice I'm gone, will you, you're so busy at the old hospital.'

But all this came much later, in the trial and in the Hallam Saul book. The first days (and the first chapters) were occupied with the killing of those four other women.

Wendy Cutforth was young, married, a teacher at a school in Ladeley. She went to work by bus from her home in Wrexlade, four miles away. In February, at four o'clock dusk, she got off the bus at Wrexlade Cross to walk to her bungalow a quarter of a mile away. She was never seen alive again, except presumably by Brannel, and her strangled body was found at ten that night in a ditch near the bus stop.

Fear of being out alone which had seized Wrexlade women after Wendy's death died down within three or four weeks. Maureen Hunter, who was only sixteen, quarrelled with her boyfriend after a dance at Wrexlade village hall and set off to walk home to Ingleford on her own. She never reached it. Her body was found in the small hours only a few yards from where Wendy's had been. Mrs Ann Daly, a middle-aged widow, also of Ingleford, had a hairdressing business in Chelmsford and drove herself to work each day via Wrexlade. Her car was found abandoned, all four doors wide open, her body in a small wood between the villages. An unsuccessful attempt had been made to bury it in the leaf mould.

Every man between sixteen and seventy in the whole of that area of Essex was closely examined by the police. Brannel was questioned, as was his father, and was released after ten minutes, having aroused no interest. In May, twenty-seven days after the death of Ann Daly, Mary Trenthyde, thirty-year-old mother of two small daughters and herself the daughter of Brannel's employer, Mark Stokes of Cross Farm, disappeared from her home during the course of a morning. One of her children was with its grandmother, the other in its pram just inside the garden gate. Mary vanished without trace, without announcing to anyone that she was going out or where she was going. A massive hunt was mounted and her strangled body finally found at midnight in a disused well half a mile away.

All these deaths took place in the spring of 1953.

The Lestranges had a flat in London not far from the Royal Free Hospital. They were not well off but Norah had a rich father who was in the habit of giving her handsome presents. One of these, for her twenty-fifth birthday, was a Triumph Alpine sports car. Michael had a car too, the kind of thing that is called an 'old banger'.

As frontispiece to Miss Hallam Saul's book is a portrait photograph of Norah Lestrange as she appeared a few months before her death. The face is oval, the features almost too perfectly symmetrical, the skin flawless and opaque. Her thick dark hair is dressed in the high fashion of the time, in short smooth curls. Her make-up is heavy and the dark, greasy lipstick coats the parted lips in a way that is somehow lascivious. The eyes stare with a humourless complacency.

Michael was furiously, painfully jealous of her. When, after they had been married six months, she began a flirtation with his best friend, a flirtation which soon developed into a love affair, he threatened to leave her, to divorce her, to lock her up, to kill Tony. She was supremely confident he would do none of these things. She talked to him. Reasonably and gently and lovingly she put it to him that it was he whom she loved and Tony with whom she was amusing herself.

'I *love* you, darling, don't you understand? This thing with Tony is just — fun. We have fun and then we say goodbye till next time and I come home to you, where my real happiness is.'

'You promised to be faithful to me,' he said, 'to forsake all others and keep only to me.'

'But I do keep only to you, darling. You have all my trust and my thoughts — Tony just has this tiny share in a very unimportant aspect of me.'

After Tony there was Philip. And after Philip, for a while, there was no one. Michael believed Norah might have tired of the 'fun' and be settling for the real happiness. He was working hard at the time for his Fellowship of the Royal College of Surgeons.

That Fellowship he got, of course, in 1952. He was surgical registrar at a big London hospital, famous for successes in the field of cardiac surgery, when the first of the Wrexlade murders took place. Wendy Cutforth. Round about the time the account of that murder and of the hunt for the Wrexlade strangler appeared in the papers, Norah met Jan Vandepeer.

Michael wasn't a reader of the popular press and the Lestranges had no television. Television wasn't, in those days, the indispensable adjunct to domestic life it has since become. Michael listened sometimes to the radio, he read *The Times*. He knew of the first of the Wrexlade murders but he wasn't much interested in it. He was busy in his job and he had Jan Vandepeer to worry about too.

The nature of the Dutchman's business in London was never clear to Michael, perhaps because it was never clear to Norah. It seemed to have something to do with commodity markets and Michael was convinced it was shady, not quite above board. Norah used to say that he was a smuggler, and she found the possibility he might be a diamond smuggler exciting. She met him on the boat coming from The Hook to Harwich after spending a week in The Hague with her parents, her father having a diplomatic post there.

'Darling, I absolutely have to have Jan, I'm crazy about him. It's nothing to do with us, though, you do see that, don't you? No one could ever take me away from you.'

He used to come over about once a month with his car and drive down to London through Colchester and Chelmsford, spend the night somewhere, carry out his business the following day and get the evening boat back. Whether he stayed in Chelmsford rather than London because it was cheaper or because Chelmsford, in those days, still kept its pleasant rural aspect, does not seem to be known. It hardly matters. Norah Lestrange was more than willing to drive the forty or so miles to Chelmsford in her Alpine and await the arrival of her dashing, blond smuggler at the Murrey Gryphon Hotel.

Chelmsford is the county town of Essex, standing on the banks of the river Chelmer and in the midst of a pleasant, though featureless, arable countryside. The land is rather flat, the fields wide, and there are many trees and numerous small woods. Wrexlade lies some four miles to the north of the town, Ingleford a little way further west. It was some time before the English reader of newspapers began to think of Wrexlade as anywhere near Chelmsford. It was simply Wrexlade, a place no one had heard of till Wendy Cutforth and then Maureen Hunter died there, a name on a map or maybe a signpost till the stranglings began — and then, gradually, a word synonymous with fascinating horror.

Bismarck Road, Hilldrop Crescent, Rillington Place — who can say now, except the amateur of crime, which of London's murderers lived in those streets? Yet in their day they were names on everyone's lips. Such is the English sense of humour that there were even jokes about them. There were jokes, says Miss Hallam Saul, about Wrexlade,

sick jokes for the utterance of one of which a famous come-
dian was banned by the BBC. Something on the lines of
what a good idea it would be to take one's mother-in-law to
Wrexlade. . .

Chelmsford, being so close to Wrexlade, became public
knowledge when Mrs Daly died. She was last seen locking
up her shop in the town centre and getting into her car. It
was after this that Norah said to Michael: 'When I'm in
Chelmsford, darling, I promise you I won't go out alone after dark.'

It was presumably to be a consolation to him that if she
went out after dark it would be in the company of Jan
Vandepeer.

Did he passively acquiesce, then, in this infidelity of
hers? In not leaving her, in being at the flat when she returned home, in continuing to be seen with her socially, he
did acquiesce. In continuing to love her in spite of himself,
he acquiesced. But his misery was terrible. He was ill with
jealousy. All his time, when he was not at the hospital,
when he was not snatching a few hours of sleep, was spent
in thrashing out in his mind what he should do. It was impossible to go on like this. If he remained in her company he
was afraid he would do her some violence, but the thought
of being permanently parted from her was horrible. When he
contemplated it he seemed to feel the solid ground sliding
away from under his feet, he felt like Othello felt — 'If I
love thee not, chaos is come again.'

In June, on Friday, 19 June, Norah went down to Chelmsford, to the Murrey Gryphon Hotel, to spend the night with
Jan Vandepeer.

Michael, who had worked every day without a break at
the hospital for two weeks, had two days off, the Friday and
the Saturday. He was tired almost to the point of sickness,
but those two days he was to have off loomed large and
glowing and inviting before him at the end of the week. He
got them out of proportion. He told himself that if he could

have those two days off to spend alone with Norah, to take
Norah somewhere into the country and laze those two days
away with her, to walk with her hand in hand down country
lanes (that he thought with such maudlin romanticism is evidence of his extreme exhaustion), if he could do that, all
would miraculously become well. He would explain and she
would explain and they would listen to each other and, in the
words of the cliché, make a fresh start. Michael was convinced of all this. He was a little mad with tiredness.

After she was dead, and they came in the morning to tell
him of her death, he took time off work. Miss Hallam Saul
gives the period as three weeks and she is probably correct.
Without those weeks of rest Michael Lestrange would very
likely have had a mental breakdown or — even worse to his
way of thinking — have killed a patient on the operating
table. So when it is said that Norah's death, though so terrible to him, saved his sanity and his career, this is not too far
from the truth. And then, when he eventually returned to his
work, he threw himself into it with total dedication. He had
nothing else, you see, nothing at all but his work for the rest
of his life that ended in the North Atlantic last March.

Brannel had nothing either. It is very difficult for the educated middle-class person, the kind of person we really
mean when we talk about 'the man in the street', to understand the lives of people like Kenneth Edward Brannel and
his father. They had no hobbies, no interests, no skill, no
knowledge in their heads, virtually no friends. Old Brannel
could read. Tracing along the lines with his finger, he could
just about make out the words in a newspaper. Kenneth
Brannel could not read at all. These days they would have
television, not then. Romantic town-dwellers imagine such
as the Brannels tending their cottage gardens, growing vege-
tables, occupying themselves with a little carpentry or shoe-
making in the evenings, cooking country stews and baking
bread. The Brannels, who worked all day in another man's
fields, would not have dreamt of further tilling the soil in the

evenings. Neither of them had ever so much as put up a shelf or stuck a sole on a boot. They lived on tinned food and fish and chips, and when the darkness came down they went to bed. There was no electricity in their cottage, anyway, and no running water or indoor sanitation. It would never have occurred to Mr Stokes of Cross Farm to provide these amenities or to the Brannels to demand them.

Downstairs in the cottage was a living room with a fireplace and a kitchen with a range. Upstairs was old Brannel's room into which the stairs went, and through the door from this room was the bedroom and only private place of Kenneth Edward Brannel. There, in a drawer in the old, wooden-knobbed tallboy, unpolished since Ellen Brannel's death, he kept his souvenirs: Wendy Cutforth's bracelet, a lock of Maureen Hunter's red hair, Ann Daly's green silk scarf, Mary Trenthyde's handkerchief with the lipstick stain and the embroidered M. The small, square handbag mirror was always assumed to have been the property of Norah Lestrange, to be a memento of her, but this was never proved. Certainly, there was no mirror in her handbag when her body was found.

In Miss Hallam Saul's *The Wrexlade Monster* there were several pictures of Brannel, a snapshot taken by his aunt when he was ten, a class group at Ingleford Middle School (which he should properly have never, with his limitations, been allowed to attend), a portrait by a Chelmsford photographer that his mother had had taken the year before her death. He was very tall, a gangling, bony man with a bumpy, tortured-looking forehead and thick, pale, curly hair. The eyes seem to say to you: The trouble is that I am puzzled, I am bewildered, I don't understand the world or you or myself and I live always in a dark mist. But when, for a little, that mist clears, look what I do. . .

His hands, hanging limply at his sides, are turned slightly, the palms half-showing, as if in helplessness and despair.

Miss Hallam Saul includes no picture of Sir Michael Lestrange, MD, FRCS, eminent cardiac specialist, author of *The
Heart,* Physician to Her Royal Highness the Duchess of
Albany, professor of cardiology at St Joachim's Hospital.
He was a thin, dark young man in those days, slight of figure and always rather shabbily dressed. One would not have
given him a second glance. Very different he was then from
the Sir Michael who was mourned by the medical elite of
two continents and whose austere yet tranquil face with its
sleek silver hair, calm light eyes and aquiline features appeared on the front pages of the world's newspapers. He had
changed more than most men in twenty-seven years. It was a
total metamorphosis, not merely an ageing.

At the time of the murder of his wife Norah he was
twenty-six. He was ambitious but not inordinately so. The
ambition, the vocation one might well call it, came later, after she was dead. He was worn out with work on 19 June
1953, and he was longing to get away to the country with his
wife and to rest.

'But, darling, I'm sure I told you. I'm going to meet Jan
at the Murrey Gryphon. I did tell you, I never have any secrets from you, you know that. *You* didn't tell me you were
going to have two days off. How was I to know? You never
seem to take time off these days and I do like to have *some*
fun *some*times.'

'Don't go,' he said.

'But, darling, I want to see Jan.'

'It's more than I can bear, the way we live,' he said. 'If
you won't stop seeing this man I shall stop you.'

He buried his face in his hands and presently she came
and laid a hand on his shoulder. He jumped up and struck
her a blow across the face. When she left for Chelmsford to
meet Jan Vandepeer she had a bruise on her cheek which she
did her best to disguise with make-up.

They had a message for her at the hotel when she got
there, from her 'husband' in Holland to say he had been de-

layed at The Hook. Hotels, in those days, were inclined to be particular that couples who shared bedrooms should at least pretend to be husband and wife. It was insinuated at Brannel's trial that Jan Vandepeer failed to arrive on this occasion because he was growing tired of Norah, but there was no evidence to support this. He was genuinely delayed and unable to leave.

Why didn't she go back to London? Perhaps she was afraid to face Michael. Perhaps she hoped Vandepeer would still come, since the phone message had been received at four-thirty. She dined alone and went out for a walk. To pick up a man, insisted prosecuting counsel, though he was not prosecuting *her* and the Old Bailey is not a court of morals. Nobody saw her go and no one seems to have been sure where she went. Eventually, of course, to Wrexlade.

Brannel also went out for a walk. The long light evenings disquieted him because he could not go to bed and he had nothing to do but sit with his father while the old man puzzled out the words in the evening paper. He went first to his bedroom to look at and handle the secret things he kept there, the scarf and the lock of hair and the bracelet and the handkerchief with M on it for Mary Trenthyde, and then he went out for his walk. Along the narrow lanes, to stop sometimes and stand, to lean over a gate, or to kick a pebble aimlessly ahead of him, dribbling it slowly from side to side of the long, straight, lonely road.

Did Norah Lestrange walk all the way to Wrexlade or did someone give her a lift and for reasons unknown abandon her there? She could have walked, it is no more than two miles from the Murrey Gryphon to the spot where her body was found half an hour before midnight. Miss Hallam Saul suggests that she was friendly with a second man in the Chelmsford neighbourhood and, in the absence of Vandepeer, set off to meet him that evening. Unlikely though that seems, similar suggestions were put forward in court. It was as if they all said, a woman like that, a woman so immoral, so promiscuous, so lacking in all proper feeling, a woman like that will do anything.

Her body was found by two young Wrexlade men going home after an evening spent at the White Swan on the Ladeley-Wrexlade road. They phoned the police from the call box on the opposite side of the lane, and the first place the police went to, because it was the nearest habitation, was the Brannels' cottage. Norah Lestrange's body lay half-hidden in long grass on the verge by the bridge over the river Lade, and the Brannels' home, Lade Cottage, was a hundred yards the other side of the bridge. They went there initially only to ask the occupants if they had seen or heard anything untoward that evening.

Old Brannel came down in his nightshirt with a coat over it. He hadn't been asleep when the police came, he said, he had been awakened a few minutes before by his son coming in. The detective superintendent looked at Kenneth Edward Brannel, at his huge dangling hands, as he stood leaning against the wall, his eyes bewildered, his mouth a little open. No, he couldn't say where he had been, round and about, up and down, he couldn't say more.

They searched the house, although they had no warrant. Much was made of this by the defence at the trial. In Kenneth Brannel's bedroom, in the drawer of the tallboy, they found Wendy Cutforth's bracelet, Maureen Hunter's lock of red hair, Ann Daly's green silk scarf, and the handkerchief with M on it for Mary Trenthyde. The Wrexlade Monster had been caught at last. They cautioned Brannel and charged him and he looked at them in a puzzled way and said: 'I don't think I killed the lady. I don't remember. But maybe I did, I forget things and it's like a mist comes up. . .'

Michael Lestrange was told of the death of his wife in the early hours of the morning. Their purpose in coming to him was to tell him the news and ask him if he would later go with them to Chelmsford formally to identify his wife's body. They asked him no questions and would have expressed their sympathy and left him in peace, had he not declared that it was he who had killed Norah and that he wanted to make a full confession.

They had no choice after that but to drive him at once to Chelmsford and take a statement from him. No one believed it. The detective chief superintendent in charge of the case was very kind to him, very gentle but firm.

'But if I tell you I killed her you must believe me. I can prove it.'

'Can you, Dr Lestrange?'

'My wife was constantly unfaithful to me. . .'

'Yes, so you have told me. And you bore with her treatment of you because of your great affection for her. The truth seems to be, doctor, that you were a devoted husband and your wife — well, a less than ideal wife.'

Michael Lestrange insisted that he had driven to Chelmsford in pursuit of Norah, intending to appeal to Jan Vandepeer to leave her alone. He had not gone into the hotel. By chance he had encountered her walking aimlessly along a Chelmsford street as he was on his way to the Murrey Gryphon.

'Mrs Lestrange was still having her dinner at the time you mention,' said Chief Superintendent Masters.

'What does that matter? It was earlier or later, I can't be precise about times. She got into the car beside me. I drove off, I don't know where, I didn't want a scene in the hotel. She told me she had to get back, she was expecting Vandepeer at any moment.'

'Vandepeer had sent her a message he wasn't coming. She didn't tell you that?'

'Is it important?' He was impatient to get his confession over. 'It doesn't matter what she told me. I can't remember what we said.'

'Can you remember where you went?'

'Of course I can't. I don't know the place. I just drove and parked somewhere, I don't know where, and we got out and walked and she drove me mad, the things she said, and I got hold of her throat and. . .' He put his head in his hands. 'I can't remember what happened next. I don't know where it was or when. I was so tired and I was mad, I think.' He looked up. 'But I killed her. If you'd like to charge me now, I'm quite ready.'

The chief superintendent said very calmly and stolidly, 'That won't be necessary, Dr Lestrange.'

Michael Lestrange shut his eyes momentarily and clenched his fists and said, 'You don't believe me.'

'I quite believe you believe it yourself, doctor.'

'Why would I confess it if it wasn't true?'

'People do, sir, it's not uncommon. Especially people like yourself who have been overworking and worrying and not getting enough sleep. You're a doctor, you know what the psychiatrists would say, that you had a reason for doing violence to your wife so that now she's dead your mind has convinced itself you killed her, and you're feeling guilt for something you had nothing to do with.

'You see, doctor, look at it from our point of view. Is it likely that you, an educated man, a surgeon, would murder anyone? Not very. And if you did, would you do it in Wrexlade? Would you do it a hundred yards from the home of a man who has murdered four other women? Would you do it by strangling with the bare hands which is the method that man always used? Would you do it four weeks after the last strangling which itself was four weeks after the previous one? Coincidences like that don't happen, do they, Dr Lestrange? But people do get overtired and suffer from stress so that they confess to crimes they never committed.'

'I bow to your superior judgement,' said Michael Lestrange.

He went to the mortuary and identified Norah's body and then he made a statement to the effect that Norah had gone to Chelmsford to meet her lover. He had last seen her at four on the previous afternoon.

Brannel was found guilty of Norah's murder, for he was specifically charged only with that, after the jury had been out half an hour. And in spite of the medical evidence as to his mental state he was condemned to death and executed a week before Christmas.

For the short time after that execution that capital punishment remained law, Michael Lestrange was bitterly opposed to it. He used to say that Brannel was a prime example of someone who had been unjustly hanged and that this must never be allowed to happen in England again. Of course there was never any doubt that Brannel had strangled Wendy Cutforth, Maureen Hunter, Ann Daly and Mary Trenthyde. The evidence was there and he repeatedly confessed to these murders. But that was not what Michael Lestrange meant. People took him to mean that a man must not be punished for committing a crime whose seriousness he is too feeble-minded to understand. This is the law, and there can be no exceptions to it merely because society wants its revenge. People took Michael Lestrange to mean that when he spoke of injustice being done to this multiple killer.

And perhaps he did.

Thornapple

The plant, which was growing up against the wall between the gooseberry bushes, stood about two feet high and had pointed, jaggedly toothed, oval leaves of a rich dark green. It bore, at the same time, a flower and a fruit. The trumpet-shaped flower had a fine, delicate texture and was of the purest white, while the green fruit, which rather resembled a chestnut though it was of a darker colour, had spines growing all over it that had a rather threatening or warning look.

According to *Indigenous British Flora*, which James held in his hand, the thornapple or Jimson's Weed or *datura stramonium* also had an unpleasant smell, but he did not find it so. What the book did not say was that *datura* was highly poisonous. James already knew that, for although this was the plant's first appearance in the Fyfields' garden, he had seen it in other parts of the village during the previous summer. And then he had only had to look at it for some adult to come rushing up and warn him of its dangers, as if he were likely at his age to eat a spiky object that looked more like a sea urchin than a seed head. Adults had not only warned him and the other children, but had fallen upon the unfortunate *datura* and tugged it out of the ground with exclamations of triumph as of a dangerous job well done.

James had discovered three specimens in the garden. The thornapple had a way of springing up in unexpected places and the book described it as 'a casual in cultivated ground'. His father would not behave in the way of those village people but he would certainly have it out as soon as he spotted it. James found this understandable. But it meant that if he was going to prepare an infusion or brew of *datura* he had better get on with it. He went back thoughtfully into the house, taking no notice of his sister Rosamund who was sitting at the kitchen table reading a foreign tourists' guide to London, and returned the book to his own room.

James's room was full of interesting things. A real glory-hole, his mother called it. He was a collector and an experimenter, was James, with an enquiring, analytical mind and more than his fair share of curiosity. He had a fish tank, its air pump bubbling away, a glass box containing hawk moth caterpillars, and mice in a cage. On the walls were crustacean charts and life cycle of the frog charts and a map of the heavens. There were several hundred books, shells and dried grasses, a snakeskin and a pair of antlers (both naturally shed) and on the top shelf of the bookcase his bottles of poison. James replaced the wild flower book and, climbing on to a stool, studied these bottles with some satisfaction.

He had prepared their contents himself by boiling leaves, flowers and berries and straining off the resulting liquor. This had mostly turned out to be a dark greenish brown or else a purplish red, which rather disappointed James who had hoped for bright green or saffron yellow, these colours being more readily associated with the sinister or the evil. The bottles were labelled *conium maculatum* and *hyoscyamus niger* rather than with their common English names, for James's mother, when she came in to dust the glory-hole, would know what hemlock and henbane were. Only the one containing his prize solution, that deadly nightshade, was left unlabelled. There would be no concealing, even from those ignorant of Latin, the significance of *atropa belladonna*.

Not that James had the least intention of putting these poisons of his to use. Nothing could have been further from his mind. Indeed, they stood up there on the high shelf precisely to be out of harm's way and, even so, whenever a small child visited the house, he took care to keep his bedroom door locked. He had made the poisons from the pure, scientific motive of *seeing if it could be done*. With caution and in a similar spirit of detachment, he had gone so far as to taste, first a few drops and then half a teaspoonful of the henbane. The result had been to make him very sick and give him painful stomach cramps which necessitated sending for the doctor who diagnosed gastritis. But James had been satisfied. It worked.

In preparing his poisons, he had had to maintain a close secrecy. That is, he made sure his mother was out of the house and Rosamund too. Rosamund would not have been interested, for one plant was much the same as another to her, she shrieked when she saw the hawk moth caterpillars and her pre-eminent wish was to go and live in London. But she was not above tale-bearing. And although neither of his parents would have been cross or have punished him or peremptorily have destroyed his preparations, for they were reasonable, level-headed people, they would certainly have prevailed upon him to throw the bottles away and have lectured him and appealed to his better nature and his common sense. So if he was going to add to his collection with a potion of *datura,* it might be wise to select Wednesday afternoon when his mother was at the meeting of the Women's Institute, and then commandeer the kitchen, the oven, a saucepan and a sieve.

His mind made up, James returned to the garden with a brown paper bag into which he dropped five specimens of thornapple fruits, all he could find, and for good measure two flowers and some leaves as well. He was sealing up the top of the bag with a strip of Scotch tape when Rosamund came up the path.

'I suppose you've forgotten we've got to take those raspberries to Aunt Julie?'

James had. But since the only thing he wanted to do at that moment was boil up the contents of the bag, and that he could not do till Wednesday, he gave Rosamund his absent-minded professor look, shrugged his shoulders and said it was impossible for *him* to forget anything *she* was capable of remembering.

'I'm going to put this upstairs,' he said. 'I'll catch you up.'

The Fyfield family had lived for many years — centuries, some said — in the village of Great Sindon in Suffolk, occupying this cottage or that one, taking over small farmhouses, yeomen all, until in the early nineteen hundreds some of them had climbed up into the middle class. James's father, son of a schoolmaster, himself taught at the University of Essex at Wivenhoe, some twenty miles distant. James was already tipped for Oxford. But they were very much of the village too, were the Fyfields of Ewes Hall Farm, with ancestors lying in the churchyard and ancestors remembered on the war memorial on the village green.

The only other Fyfield at present living in Great Sindon was Aunt Julie who wasn't really an aunt but a connection by marriage, her husband having been a second cousin twice removed or something of that sort. James couldn't recall that he had ever been particularly nice to her or specially polite (as Rosamund was) but for all that Aunt Julie seemed to prefer him over pretty well everyone else. With the exception, perhaps, of Mirabel. And because she preferred him she expected him to pay her visits. Once a week these visits would have taken place if Aunt Julie had had her way, but James was not prepared to fall in with that and his parents had not encouraged it.

'I shouldn't like anyone to think James was after her money,' his mother had said.

'Everyone knows that's to go to Mirabel,' said his father.

'All the more reason. I should hate to have it said James was after Mirabel's rightful inheritance.'

Rosamund was unashamedly after it or part of it, though that seemed to have occurred to no one. She had told James so. A few thousand from Aunt Julie would help enormously in her ambition to buy herself a flat in London, for which she had been saving up since she was seven. But flats were going up in price all the time (she faithfully read the estate agents' pages in the *Observer*), her £28.50 would go nowhere, and without a windfall her situation looked hopeless. She was very single-minded, was Rosamund, and she had a lot of determination. James supposed she had picked the raspberries herself and that her 'we've got to take them' had its origins in her own wishes and was in no way a directive from their mother. But he didn't much mind going. There was a mulberry tree in Aunt Julie's garden and he would be glad of a chance to examine it. He was thinking of keeping silkworms.

It was a warm sultry day in high summer, a day of languid air and half-veiled sun, of bumble bees heavily laden and roses blown but still scented. The wood hung on the hillsides like blue smoky shadows, and the fields where they were beginning to cut the wheat were the same colour as Rosamund's hair. Very long and straight was the village street of Great Sindon, as is often the case in Suffolk. Aunt Julie lived at the very end of it in a plain, solidly built, grey brick, double-fronted house with a shallow slate roof and two tall chimneys. It would never, in the middle of the nineteenth century when it had been built, have been designated a 'gentleman's house', for there were only four bedrooms and a single kitchen, while the ceilings were low and the stairs steep, but nowadays any gentleman might have been happy to live in it and village opinion held that it was worth a very large sum of money. Sindon Lodge stood in about two acres of land which included an apple orchard, a lily pond and a large lawn on which the mulberry tree was.

James and his sister walked along in almost total silence. They had little in common and it was hot, the air full of tiny insects that came off the harvest fields. James knew that he had only been invited to join her because if she had gone alone Aunt Julie would have wanted to know where he was and would have sulked and probably not been at all welcoming. He wondered if she knew that the basket in which she had put the raspberries, having first lined it with a white paper table napkin, was in fact of the kind that is intended for wine, being made with a loop of cane at one end to hold the neck of the bottle. She had changed, he noticed, from her jeans into her new cotton skirt, the Laura Ashley print, and had brushed her wheat-coloured hair and tied a black velvet ribbon round it. Much good it would do her, thought James, but he decided not to tell her the true function of the basket unless she did anything particular to irritate him.

But as they were passing the church Rosamund suddenly turned to face him and asked him if he knew Aunt Julie now had a lady living with her to look after her. A companion, this person was called, said Rosamund. James hadn't known — he had probably been absorbed in his own thoughts when it was discussed — and he was somewhat chagrined.

'So what?'

'So nothing. Only I expect she'll open the door to us. You didn't know, did you? It isn't true you know things I don't. I often know things you don't, I *often* do.'

James did not deign to reply.

'She said that if ever she got so she *had* to have someone living with her, she'd get Mirabel to come. And Mirabel wanted to, she actually liked the idea of living in the country. But Aunt Julie didn't ask her, she got this lady instead, and I heard Mummy say Aunt Julie doesn't want Mirabel in

the house any more. I don't know why. Mummy said maybe
Mirabel won't get Aunt Julie's money now.'

James whistled a few bars from the overture to the *Barber
of Seville*. 'I know why.'

'Bet you don't.'

'O.K., so I don't.'

'Why, then?'

'You're not old enough to understand. And, incidentally,
you may not know it but that thing you've got the raspberries in is a wine basket.'

The front door of Sindon Lodge was opened to them by a
fat woman in a cotton dress with a wrap-around overall on
top of it. She seemed to know who they were and said she
was Mrs Crowley but they could call her Auntie Elsie if they
liked. James and Rosamund were in silent agreement that
they did not like. They went down the long passage where it
was rather cold even on the hottest day.

Aunt Julie was in the room with the french windows, sitting in a chair looking into the garden, the grey cat Palmerston on her lap. Her hair was exactly the same colour as
Palmerston's fur and nearly as fluffy. She was a little wiz-
ened woman, very old, who always dressed in jumpers and
trousers which, James thought privately, made her look a bit
like a monkey. Arthritis twisted and half-crippled her,
slowly growing worse, which was probably why she had engaged Mrs Crowley.

Having asked Rosamund why she had put the raspberries
in a wine basket — she must be sure to take it straight back
to Mummy — Aunt Julie turned her attention to James, demanding of him what he had been collecting lately, how
were the hawk moth caterpillars and what sort of a school report had he had at the end of the summer term? A further ten
minutes of this made James, though not unusually tender-
hearted towards his sister, actually feel sorry for Rosamund,
so he brought himself to tell Aunt Julie that she had passed

her piano exam with distinction and, if he might be excused, he would like to go out and look at the mulberry tree.

The garden had a neglected look and in the orchard tiny apples, fallen during the 'June drop', lay rotting in the long grass. There were no fish in the pond and had not been for years. The mulberry tree was loaded with sticky-looking squashy red fruit, but James supposed that silkworms fed only on the leaves. Would he be allowed to help himself to mulberry leaves? Deciding that he had a lot to learn about the rearing of silkworms, he walked slowly round the tree, remembering now that it was Mirabel who had first identified the tree for him and had said how wonderful she thought it would be to make one's own silk.

It seemed to him rather dreadful that just because Mirabel had had a baby she might be deprived of all this. For 'all this', the house, the gardens, the vaguely huge sum of money which Uncle Walter had made out of building houses and had left to his widow, was surely essential to poor Mirabel who made very little as a free-lance designer and must have counted on it.

Had he been alone, he might have raised the subject with Aunt Julie who would take almost anything from him even though she called him an *enfant terrible*. She sometimes said he could twist her round his little finger, which augured well for getting the mulberry leaves. But he wasn't going to talk about Mirabel in front of Rosamund. Instead, he mentioned it tentatively to his mother immediately Rosamund, protesting, had been sent to bed.

'Well, darling, Mirabel did go and have a baby without being married. And when Aunt Julie was young that was a terrible thing to do. We can't imagine, things have changed so much. But Aunt Julie has very strict ideas and she must think of Mirabel as a bad woman.'

'I see,' said James, who didn't quite. 'And when she dies Mirabel won't be in her will, is that right?'

'I don't think we ought to talk about things like that.'

'Certainly we shouldn't,' said James's father.

'No, but I want to know. You're always saying people shouldn't keep things secret from children. Has Aunt Julie made a new will, cutting Mirabel out?'

'She hasn't made a will at all, that's the trouble. According to the law, a great niece doesn't automatically inherit if a person dies intestate — er, that is, dies. . .'

'I know what intestate means,' said James.

'So I suppose Mirabel thought she could get her to make a will. It doesn't sound very nice put like that but, really, why shouldn't poor Mirabel have it? If she doesn't, I don't believe there's anyone else near enough and it will just go to the state.'

'Shall we change the subject now?' said James's father.

'Yes, all right,' said James. 'Will you be going to the Women's Institute the same as usual on Wednesday?'

'Of course I will, darling. Why on earth do you ask?'

'I just wondered,' said James.

James's father was on holiday while the university was down and on the following day he went out into the fruit garden with a basket and his weeder and uprooted the thornapple plant that was growing between the gooseberry bushes. James, sitting in his bedroom, reading *The Natural History of Selborne,* watched him from the window. His father put the thornapple on the compost heap and went hunting for its fellows, all of which he found in the space of five minutes. James sighed but took this destruction philosophically. He had enough in the brown paper bag for his needs.

As it happened, he had the house to himself for the making of his newest brew. His father announced at lunch that he would be taking the car into Bury St Edmunds that afternoon and both children could come with him if they wanted to. Rosamund did. Bury, though not London, was at any rate a sizeable town with plenty of what she liked, shops and restaurants and cinemas and crowds. Once alone, James chose an enamel saucepan of the kind which looked as if all traces of *datura* could easily be removed from it afterwards, put into it about a pint of water and set this to boil. Meanwhile, he cut up the green spiny fruits to reveal the black seeds they contained. When the water boiled he dropped in the fruit pieces and the seeds and leaves and flowers and kept it all simmering for half an hour, occasionally stirring the mixture with a skewer. Very much as he had expected, the bright green colour hadn't been maintained, but the solid matter and the liquid had all turned a dark khaki brown. James didn't dare use a sieve to strain it in case he couldn't get it clean again, so he pressed all the liquor out with his hands until nothing remained but some soggy pulp.

This he got rid of down the waste disposal unit. He poured the liquid, reduced now to not much more than half a pint, into the medicine bottle he had ready for it, screwed on the cap and labelled it: *datura stramonium*. The pan he scoured thoroughly but a few days later, when he saw that his mother had used it for boiling the peas they were about to eat with their fish for supper, he half-expected the whole family to have griping pains and even tetanic convulsions. But nothing happened and no one suffered any ill effects.

By the time the new school term started James had produced a substance he hoped might be muscarine from boiling up the fly agaric fungus and some rather doubtful cyanide from apricot kernels. There were now ten bottles of poison on the top shelf of his bookcases. But no one was in the least danger from them, and even when the Fyfield household was increased by two members there was no need for James to keep his bedroom door locked, for Mirabel's little boy was only six months old and naturally as yet unable to walk.

Mirabel's arrival had been entirely impulsive. A ridiculous way to behave, James's father said. The lease of her flat in Kensington was running out and instead of taking steps to find herself somewhere to live, she had waited until the

lease was within a week of expiry and had turned up in Great
Sindon to throw herself on the mercy of Aunt Julie. She
came by taxi from Ipswich station, lugging a suitcase and
carrying the infant Oliver.

Mrs Crowley had opened the door to her and Mirabel had
never got as far as seeing Aunt Julie. A message was
brought back to say she was not welcome at Sindon Lodge
as her aunt thought she had made clear enough by telephone
and letter. Mirabel, who had believed that Aunt Julie would
soften at the sight of her, had a choice between going back to
London, finding a hotel in Ipswich or taking refuge with the
Fyfields. She told the taxi to take her to Ewes Hall Farm.

'How could I turn her away?' James heard his mother say.
Mirabel was upstairs putting Oliver to bed. 'There she was
on the doorstep with that great heavy case and the baby
screaming his head off, poor mite. And she's such a little
scrap of a thing.'

James's father had been gloomy ever since he got home.
'Mirabel is exactly the sort of person who would come for
the weekend and stay ten years.'

'No one would stay here for ten years if they could live in
London,' said Rosamund.

In the event, Mirabel didn't stay ten years, though she
was still there after ten weeks. And on almost every day of
those ten weeks she tried in vain to get her foot in the door of
Sindon Lodge. Whoever happened to be in the living room
of Ewes Hall Farm in the evening — and in the depths of
winter that was usually everyone — was daily regaled with
Mirabel's grievances against life and with denunciations of
the people who had injured her, notably Oliver's father and
Aunt Julie. James's mother sometimes said that it was sad
for Oliver having to grow up without a father, but since Mirabel never mentioned him without saying how selfish he
was, the most immature, heartless, mean, lazy and cruel
man in London, James thought Oliver would be better off

without him. As for Aunt Julie, she must be senile, Mirabel
said, she must have lost her wits.

'Can you imagine anyone taking such an attitude, Elizabeth, in this day and age? She literally will not have me in
the house because I've got Oliver and I wasn't married to
Francis. Thank God I wasn't, that's all I can say. But
wouldn't you think that sort of thing went out with the dark
ages?'

'She'll come round in time,' said James's mother.

'Yes, but how much time? I mean, she hasn't got that
much, has she? And here am I taking shameful advantage of
your hospitality. You don't know how guilty it makes me,
only I literally have nowhere to go. And I simply cannot afford to take another flat like the last, frankly, I couldn't raise
the cash. I haven't been getting the contracts like I used to
before Oliver was born and of course I've never had a penny
from that unspeakable, selfish, pig of a man.'

James's mother and father would become very bored with
all this but they could hardly walk out of the room. James
and Rosamund could, though after a time Mirabel took to
following James up to the glory-hole where she would sit on
his bed and continue her long, detailed, repetitive com-
plaints just as if he were her own contemporary.

It was a little disconcerting at first, though he got used to
it. Mirabel was about thirty but to him and his sister she
seemed the same age as their parents, middle-aged, old,
much as anyone did who was over, say, twenty-two. And
till he got accustomed to her manner he hardly knew what to
make of the way she gazed intensely into his eyes or suddenly clutched him by the arm. She described herself (fre-
quently) as passionate, nervous and highly strung.

She was a small woman and James was already taller than
she. She had a small, rather pinched face with large promi-
nent dark eyes and she wore her long hair hanging loose like
Rosamund's. The Fyfields were big-boned, fair-headed
people with ruddy skins but Mirabel was dark and very thin

and her wrists and hands and ankles and feet were very slender and narrow. There was, of course, no blood relationship, Mirabel being Aunt Julie's own sister's granddaughter.

Mirabel was not her baptismal name. She had been christened Brenda Margaret but it had to be admitted that the name she had chosen for herself suited her better, suited her feyness, her intense smiles and brooding sadnesses, and the clinging clothes she wore, the muslins and the trailing shawls. She always wore a cloak or a cape to go into the village and James's mother said she couldn't remember Mirabel ever having possessed a coat.

James had always had rather a sneaking liking for her, he hadn't known why. But now that he was older and saw her daily, he understood something he had not known before. He liked Mirabel, he couldn't help himself, because she seemed to like him so much and because she flattered him. It was funny, he could listen to her flattery and distinguish it for what it was, but this knowledge did not detract a particle from the pleasure he felt in hearing it.

'You're absolutely brilliant for your age, aren't you, James?' Mirabel would say. 'I suppose you'll be a professor one day. You'll probably win the Nobel prize.'

She asked him to teach her things: how to apply Pythagoras' Theorem, how to convert Fahrenheit temperatures into Celsius, ounces into grammes, how to change the plug on her hair dryer.

'I'd like to think Oliver might have half your brains, James, and then I'd be quite content. Francis is clever, mind you, though he's so immature and lazy with it. I literally think *you're* more mature than he is.'

Aunt Julie must have known for a long time that Mirabel was staying with the Fyfields, for nothing of that kind could be concealed in a village of the size of Great Sindon, but it was December before she mentioned the matter to James. They were sitting in front of the fire in the front sitting room

at Sindon Lodge, eating crumpets toasted by Mrs Crowley
and drinking Earl Grey tea, while Palmerston stretched out
on the hearth rug. Outside a thin rain was driving against the
window panes.

'I hope Elizabeth knows what she's doing, that's all. If
you're not careful you'll all be stuck with that girl for life.'

James said nothing.

'Of course you don't understand the ins and outs of it at
your age, but in my opinion your parents should have
thought twice before they let her come into their home and
bring her illegitimate child with her.' Aunt Julie looked at
him darkly and perhaps spitefully. 'That could have a
very bad effect on Rosamund, you know. Rosamund will
think immoral behaviour is quite all right when she sees people like Mirabel getting rewarded for it.'

'She's not exactly *rewarded*,' said James, starting on the
tea cakes and the greengage jam. 'We don't give her anything but her food and she has to sleep in the same room as
Oliver.' This seemed to him by far the worst aspect of Mirabel's situation.

Aunt Julie made no reply. After a while she said, looking
into the fire, 'How d'you think you'd feel if you knew people only came to see you for the sake of getting your money?
That's all Madam Mirabel wants. She doesn't care for me,
she couldn't care less. She comes here sweet talking to Mrs
Crowley because she thinks once she's in here I'll take her
back and make a will leaving everything I've got to her and
that illegitimate child of hers. How d'you think you'd like
it? Maybe you'll come to it yourself one day, your grandchildren sucking up to you for what they can get.'

'You don't *know* people come for that,' said James awk-
wardly, thinking of Rosamund.

Aunt Julie made a sound of disgust. 'Aaah!' She struck
out with her arthritic hand as if pushing something away.
'I'm not green, am I? I'm not daft. I'd despise myself, I can

tell you, if I pretended it wasn't as plain as the nose on my face what you all come for.'

The fire crackled and Palmerston twitched in his sleep.

'Well, I don't,' said James.

'Don't you now, Mr Pure-and-holy?'

James grinned. 'There's a way you could find out. You could make a will and leave your money to other people and tell me I wasn't getting any — and then see if I'd still come.'

'I could, could I? You're so sharp, James Fyfield, you'll cut yourself badly one of these fine days.'

Her prophecy had a curious fulfilment that same evening. James, groping about on the top shelf of his bookcase, knocked over the bottle of muscarine and cut his hand on the broken glass. It wasn't much of a cut but the stuff that had been inside the bottle got onto it and gave him a very uncomfortable and anxious hour. Nothing happened, his arm didn't swell up or go black or anything of that sort, but it made him think seriously about the other nine bottles remaining. Wasn't it rather silly to keep them? That particular interest of his, no longer compelling, he was beginning to see as childish. Besides, with Oliver in the house, Oliver who was crawling now and would soon walk, to keep the poisons might be more than dangerous, it might be positively criminal.

His mind made up, he took the bottles down without further vacillation and one by one poured their contents away down his bedroom washbasin. Some of them smelt dreadful. The henbane smelt like the inside of his mouse cage when he hadn't cleaned it out for a day.

He poured them all away with one exception. He couldn't quite bring himself to part with the *datura*. It had always been his pride, better even than the nightshade. Sometimes he had sat there at his desk, doing his homework, and glanced up at the *datura* bottle and wondered what people would think if they had known he had the means in his bedroom to dispose of (probably) half the village. He looked at it now, recalling how he had picked the green spiny thornapples in the nick of time before his father had up-rooted all the beautiful and sinister plants — he looked at it and replaced it on the top shelf. Then he sat down at the desk and did his Latin unseen.

Mirabel was still with them at Christmas. On Christmas Eve she carried up to Sindon Lodge the pale blue jumper, wrapped in holly-patterned paper, the two-pound box of chocolates and the poinsettia in a golden pot she had bought for Aunt Julie. And she took Rosamund with her. Rosamund wore her new scarlet coat with the white fur which was a Christmas present in advance, and the scarf with Buckingham Palace and the Tower of London printed on it which was another, and Mirabel wore her dark blue cloak and her angora hat and very high-heeled grey suede boots that skidded dangerously about on the ice. Oliver was left behind in the care of James's mother.

But if Mirabel had thought that the presence of Rosamund would provide her with an entrée to the house she was mistaken. Mrs Crowley, with a sorrowful expression, brought back the message that Aunt Julie could see no one. She had one of her gastric attacks, she was feeling very unwell, and she never accepted presents when she had nothing to give in return. Mirabel read a great deal, perhaps more than had been intended, into this valedictory shot.

'She means she'll never have anything to give me,' she said, sitting on James's bed. 'She means she's made up her mind not to leave me anything.'

It was a bit — James sought for the word and found it — a bit *degrading* to keep hanging on like this for the sake of money you hadn't earned and had no real right to. But he knew better than to say something so unkind and moralistic. He suggested tentatively that Mirabel might feel happier if she went back to her designing of textiles and forgot about Aunt Julie and her will. She turned on him in anger.

'What do you know about it? You're only a child. You

don't know what I've suffered with that selfish brute of a
man. I was left all alone to have my baby, I might have been
literally destitute for all he cared, left to bring Oliver up on
my own and without a roof over my head. How can I work?
What am I supposed to do with Oliver? Oh, it's so unfair.
Why shouldn't I get her money? It's not as if I was depriving
anyone else, it's not as if she'd left it to someone and I was
trying to get her to change anything. If I don't get it, it'll just
go to the government.'

Mirabel was actually crying by now. She wiped her eyes
and sniffed. 'I'm sorry, James, I shouldn't take it out on
you. I think I'm just getting to the end of my tether.'

James's father had used those very words earlier in the
day. He was getting to the end of his tether as far as Mirabel
was concerned. Once get Christmas over and then, if
James's mother wouldn't tell her she had outstayed her welcome, he would. Let her make things up with that chap of
hers, Oliver's father, or get rooms somewhere or move in
with one of those arty London friends. She wasn't even a re-
lation, he didn't even like her, and she had now been with
them for nearly three months.

'I know I can't go on staying here,' said Mirabel to James
when hints had been dropped, 'but where am I to go?' She
cast her eyes heavenwards or at least as far as the top shelf of
the bookcase where they came to rest on the bottle of
greenish-brown liquid labelled: *datura stramonium*.

'What on earth's that?' said Mirabel. 'What's in that bottle? *Datura* whatever-it-is, I can't pronounce it. It isn't
cough mixture, is it? It's such a horrible colour.'

Six months before, faced with that question, James would
have prevaricated or told a lie. But now he felt differently
about those experiments of his, and he also had an obscure
feeling that if he told Mirabel the truth and she told his
mother, he would be forced to do something his own will refused to compel him to and throw the bottle away.

'Poison,' he said laconically.

'Poison?'

'I made it out of something called Jimson's Weed or thornapple. It's quite concentrated. I think a dose of it might be lethal.'

'Were you going to kill mice with it or something?'

James would not have dreamt of killing a mouse or, indeed, any animal. It exasperated him that Mirabel who ought to have known him quite well, who had lived in the same house with him and talked to him every day, should have cared so little about him and been so uninterested in his true nature as not to be aware of this.

'I wasn't going to kill anything with it. It was just an experiment.'

Mirabel gave a hollow ringing laugh. 'Would it kill me? Maybe I'll come up here while you're at school and take that bottle and — and put an end to myself. It would be a merciful release, wouldn't it? Who'd care? Not a soul. Not Francis, not Aunt Julie. They'd be glad. There's not a soul in the world who'd miss me.'

'Well, Oliver would,' said James.

'Yes, my darling little boy would, my Oliver would care. People don't realize I only want Aunt Julie's money for Oliver. It's not for me. I just want it to give Oliver a chance in life.' Mirabel looked at James, her eyes narrowing. 'Sometimes I think you're the only person on earth Aunt Julie cares for. I bet if you said to her to let bygones be bygones and have me back, she'd do it. I bet she would. She'd even make a will if you suggested it. I suppose it's because you're clever. She admires intellectuals.'

'If I suggested she make a will in Oliver's favour, I reckon she just might,' said James. 'He's her great-great-nephew, isn't he? That's quite a good idea, she might do that.'

He couldn't understand why Mirabel had suddenly become so angry, and with a shout of 'Oh, you're impossible, you're as bad as the rest of them!' had banged out of his room. Had she thought he was being sarcastic? It was obvious she wanted him to work on Aunt Julie for her and he wondered if she had flattered him simply towards this end. Perhaps. But however that might be, he could see a kind of justice in her claim. She had been a good niece, or greatniece, to Aunt Julie, a frequent visitor to Sindon Lodge before the episode of Francis, a faithful sender of birthday and Christmas cards, or so his mother said, and attentive when Aunt Julie had been ill. On the practical or selfish side, getting Mirabel accepted at Sindon Lodge would take her away from Ewes Hall Farm where her presence frayed his father's temper, wore his mother out, made Rosamund sulk and was beginning to bore even him. So perhaps he would mention it to Aunt Julie on his next visit. And he began to plan a sort of strategy, how he would suggest a meeting with Oliver, for all old people seemed to like babies, and follow it up with persuasive stuff about Oliver needing a home and money and things to make up for not having had a father. But, in fact, he had to do nothing. For Mrs Crowley had been offered a better job in a more lively place and had suddenly departed, leaving Aunt Julie stiff with arthritis and in the middle of a gastric attack.

She crawled to the door to let James in, a grotesque figure in red corduroy trousers and green jumper, her witch's face framed in a woolly fuzz of grey hair, and behind her, picking his way delicately, Palmerston with tail erect.

'You can tell that girl she can come up here tonight if she likes. She'd better bring her illegitimate child with her, I don't suppose your mother wants him.'

Aunt Julie's bark was worse than her bite. Perhaps, indeed, she had no real bite. When James next went to Sindon Lodge some three weeks later Mirabel was settled in as if she had lived there all her life, Oliver was on the hearthrug where he had usurped Palmerston's place and Aunt Julie was wearing Mirabel's Christmas present.

She hardly spoke to James while her great-niece was in

the room. She lay back in her armchair with her eyes closed
and though the young woman's clothes she wore gave to her
appearance a kind of bizarre mockery of youth, you could
see now that she was very old. Recent upheavals had aged
her. Her face looked as if it were made of screwed-up brown
paper. But when Mirabel went away — was compelled to
leave them by Oliver's insistent demands for his tea — Aunt
Julie seemed to revive. She opened her eyes and said to
James in her sharpest and most offhand tone: 'This is the last
time you'll come here, I daresay.'

'Why do you say that?'

'I've made my will, that's why, and you're not in it.'

She cocked a distorted thumb in the direction of the door.
'I've left the house and the furniture and all I've got to *her*.
And a bit to someone else we both know.'

'Who?' said James.

'Never you mind. It's not you and it's none of your business.' A curious look came into Aunt Julie's eyes. 'What
I've done is leave my money to two people I can't stand and
who don't like me. You think that's silly, don't you?
They've both sucked up to me and danced attendance on me
and told a lot of lies about caring for me. Well, I'm tired,
I'm sick of it. They can have what they want and I'll never
again have to see that look on their faces.'

'What look?'

'A kind of greedy pleading. The kind of look no one
ought to have unless she's starving. You don't know what
I'm talking about, do you? You're as clever as they come
but you don't know what life is, not yet you don't. How
could you?'

The old woman closed her eyes and there was silence in
which the topmost log crumpled and sank into the heart of
the fire with a rush of sparks, and Palmerston strode out
from where he had taken refuge from Oliver, rubbed himself
against James's legs and settled down in the red glow to
wash himself. Suddenly Aunt Julie spoke.

'I didn't want you corrupted, can you understand that? I didn't want to *spoil* the only one who means more than a row of pins to me. But I don't know . . . . If I wasn't too old to stand the fuss there'd be I'd go back on what I've done and leave the house to you. Or your mother, she's a nice woman.'

'She's got a house.'

'Houses can be sold, you silly boy. You don't suppose Madam Mirabel will *live* here, do you?' Mirabel must have heard that, James thought, as the door opened and the tea trolley appeared, but there was no warning Aunt Julie or catching her eye. 'I could make another will yet, I could bring myself to it. They say it's a woman's privilege to change her mind.'

Mirabel looked cross and there was very little chance of conversation after that as Oliver, when he was being fed or bathed or played with, dominated everything. He was a big child with reddish hair, not in the least like Mirabel but resembling, presumably, the mean and heartless Francis. He was now ten months old and walking, 'into everything', as James's mother put it, and it was obvious that he tired Aunt Julie whose expression became quite distressed when screams followed Mirabel's refusal to give him chocolate cake. Oliver's face and hands were wiped clean and he was put on the floor where he tried to eat pieces of coal out of the scuttle and, when prevented, set about tormenting the cat. James got up to go and Aunt Julie clutched his hand as he passed her, whispering with a meaning look that virtue was its own reward.

It was not long before he discovered who the 'someone else we both know' was. Aunt Julie wrote a letter to James's parents in which she told them she was leaving a sum of money to Rosamund in her will. Elizabeth Fyfield said she thought there was something very unpleasant about this letter and that it seemed to imply Rosamund had gone to Sindon Lodge with 'great expectations' in mind. She was upset by it but Rosamund was jubilant. Aunt Julie had not said what the sum was but Rosamund was sure it must be thousands and thousands of pounds — half a million was the highest figure she mentioned — and with her birthday money (she was eleven on 1 March) she bought herself a book of photographs of London architecture, mostly of streets in Mayfair, Belgravia and Knightsbridge, so that she could decide which one to have her flat in.

'I think we made a great mistake in telling her,' said James's father.

For Rosamund had taken to paying weekly visits to Sindon Lodge. She seldom went without some small gift for Aunt Julie, a bunch of snowdrops, a lop-sided pot she had made at school, a packet of peppermints.

'Wills can be changed, you know,' said James.

'That's not why I go. Don't you dare say that! I go because I love her. You're just jealous of me and you haven't been for weeks and weeks.'

It was true. He saw that Rosamund had indeed been corrupted and he, put to the test, had failed it. Yet it was not entirely disillusionment or pique which kept him from Sindon Lodge but rather a feeling that it must be wrong to manipulate people in this way. He had sometimes heard his father use the expression 'playing God' and now he understood what it meant. Aunt Julie had played God with him and with Rosamund and with Mirabel too. Probably she was still doing it, hinting at will-changing each time Mirabel displeased her. So he would go there to defy this manipulating, not to be a puppet moved by her strings, he would go on the following day on his way home from school.

But although he went as he had promised himself he would, to show her his visits were disinterested and that he could stick to his word, he never saw her alive again. The doctor's car was outside when he turned in at the gate. Mirabel let him in after he had rung the bell three times, a harassed, pale Mirabel with Oliver fretful in her arms. Aunt

Julie had had one of her gastric attacks, a terrible attack which had gone on all night. Mirabel had not known what to do and Aunt Julie had refused to let her call an ambulance, she wouldn't go into hospital. The doctor had come first thing and had come back later and was with her now.

She had had to scrub out the room and actually *burn* the sheets, Mirabel said darkly. The mess had been frightful, worse than James could possibly imagine, but she couldn't have let the doctor see her like that. Mirabel said she hoped the worst was over but she didn't look very hopeful, she looked unhappy. James went no further inside than the hall. He said to tell Aunt Julie he had been, please not to forget to tell her, and Mirabel said she wouldn't forget. He walked away slowly. Spring was in the air and the neat, symmetrical front garden of Sindon Lodge was full of daffodils, their bent heads bouncing in the breeze. At the gate he met Palmerston coming in with the corpse of a fieldmouse dangling from his mouth. Without dropping his booty, Palmerston rubbed himself against James's legs and James stroked him, feeling rather depressed.

Two days later Aunt Julie had another attack and it killed her. Or the stroke which she had afterwards killed her, the doctor said. The cause of death on the certificate was 'food poisoning and cerebral haemorrhage', according to Mrs Hodges who had been Aunt Julie's cleaner and who met James's mother in the village. Apparently on death certificates the doctor has to put down the main cause and the contributory cause, which was another piece of information for James to add to his increasing store.

James's parents went to the funeral and of course Mirabel went too. James did not want to go and it never crossed his mind that he would be allowed to on a school day, but Rosamund cried when they stopped her. She wanted to have her red and white coat dyed black and to carry a small bouquet of violets. The provisions of the will were made known during the following days, though there was no dramatic will-reading after the funeral as there is in books.

Sindon Lodge was to go to Mirabel and so was all Aunt Julie's money with the exception of Rosamund's 'bit', and bit, relatively speaking, it turned out to be. Five hundred pounds. Rosamund cried (and said she was crying because she missed Aunt Julie) and then she sulked, but when the will was proved and she actually got the money, when she was shown the cheque and it was paid into her Post Office Savings account, she cheered up and became quite sensible. She even confided to James, without tears or flounces, that it would have been a terrible responsibility to have half a million and she would always have been worried that people were only being nice to her for the sake of the money.

James got Palmerston. It was set out in the will, the cat described and mentioned by name, and bequeathed 'if the animal should survive me, to James Alexander Fyfield, of Ewes Hall Farm, Great Sindon, he being the only person I know I can trust. . .'

'What an awful thing to say,' said Mirabel. 'Imagine, literally to have a thing like that written down. I'm sure James is welcome to it. I should certainly have had it destroyed, you can't have a cat about the place with a baby.'

Palmerston had lived so long at Sindon Lodge that he was always going back there, though he kept instinctively out of Mirabel's way. For Mirabel, contrary to what Aunt Julie had predicted, did not sell the house. Nor did she make any of those changes the village had speculated about when it knew she was not going to sell. Sindon Lodge was not painted white with a blue front door or recarpeted or its kitchen fitted out with the latest gadgets. Mirabel did nothing ostentatious, made no splash and bought herself nothing but a small and modest car. For a while it seemed as if she were lying low, keeping herself to herself, mourning in fact, and James's mother said perhaps they had all misjudged her and she had really loved Aunt Julie after all.

Things began to change with the appearance on the scene of Gilbert Coleridge. Where Mirabel had met him no one seemed to know, but one day his big yellow Volvo estate car was seen outside Sindon Lodge, on the next Mirabel was seen in the passenger seat of that car, and within hours it was all over the village that she had a man friend.

'He sounds a nice, suitable sort of person,' said James's mother, whose bush telegraph system was always sound. 'Two or three years older than she and never had a wife — well, you never know these days, do you? — and already a partner in his firm. It would be just the thing for Oliver. He needs a man about the house.'

'Let's hope she has the sense to marry this one,' said James's father.

But on the whole, apart from this, the Fyfield family had lost interest in Mirabel. It had been galling for them that Mirabel, having got what she wanted with their help, first the entrée to Sindon Lodge and then the possession of it, had lost interest in *them*. She was not to be met with in the village because she scarcely walked anywhere if she could help it, and although Rosamund called several times, Mirabel was either not at home or else far too busy to ask anyone in. James overheard his mother saying that it was almost as if Mirabel felt she had said too much while she stayed with them, had shown too openly her desires, and now these were gratified, wanted as little as possible to do with those who had listened to her confidences. But it suited the Fyfields equally, for the arrival of Mirabel was always followed by trouble and by demands.

The summer was hotter and dryer than the previous one had been, and the soft fruit harvest was exceptionally good. But this year there was no Aunt Julie to cast a cynical eye over baskets of raspberries. And Jimson's Weed, *datura*, the thornapple, did not show itself in the Fyfields' garden or, apparently, in any part of Great Sindon. A 'casual,' as the wild plant book described it, it had gone in its mysterious way to ground or else wandered to some distant place away over the meadows.

Had it appeared, it would have exercised no fascination over James. He had his thirteenth birthday in June and he felt immeasurably, not just a year, older than he had done the previous summer. For one thing, he was about six inches taller, he had 'shot up' as his mother said, and sometimes the sight in a mirror of this new towering being could almost alarm him. He looked back with incredulous wonder on the child he had been, the child who had boiled noxious fruits and leaves in a pot, who had kept white mice in a cage and caterpillars in a box. He had entered his teens and was a child no more.

Perhaps it was his height that led directly to the drama — 'the absolutely worst day of my life', Rosamund called it — or it might have been Mrs Hodges's operation or even the fact, that, for once in a way, the Women's Institute met on a Tuesday rather than a Wednesday. It might have been any of those factors, though most of all it happened because Mirabel was inevitably and unchangingly Mirabel.

The inhabitants of Ewes Hall Farm knew very little about her life since they hardly ever saw her. It came as a surprise to Elizabeth Fyfield to learn how much time Mrs Hodges had been spending sitting in with Oliver or minding him in her own home. It was Mrs Hodges's daughter who told her, at the same time as she told her that her mother would be three weeks in hospital having her hysterectomy and another goodness knows how many convalescing. Mirabel would have to look elsewhere for a babysitter.

She looked, as they might have known she would, to the Fyfields.

Presenting herself on their doorstep with Oliver on one arm and a heavy shopping basket on the other, she greeted James's mother with a winsome, nervous smile. It might have been last year all over again, except that Oliver was a little boy now and no longer a baby. James, home for the long summer holidays, heard her sigh with despair and break into a long apology for having 'neglected' them for so long. The fact was she was engaged to be married. Did Elizabeth know that?

'I hope you'll be happy, Mirabel.'

'Gilbert will make a marvellous father,' said Mirabel. 'When I compare him with that stupid, immature oaf, that Francis, it just makes me — oh, well, that's all water under the bridge now. Anyway, Elizabeth dear, what I came to ask you was, do you think James or Rosamund would do some baby-sitting for me? I'd pay them the going rate, I'd pay them what I pay Mrs Hodges. Only it's so awful for me never being able to go out with my fiancé, and actually tomorrow I'm supposed to be meeting his parents for the first time. Well, I can't take a baby of Oliver's age to a dinner party, can I?'

'Rosamund's out of the question,' said James's mother, and she didn't say it very warmly. 'She's only eleven. I couldn't possibly let her have sole charge of Oliver.'

'But James would be all right, wouldn't he? James has got so *tall*, he looks almost a grown man. And James is terribly mature, anyway.'

His mother didn't answer that. She gave one of those sighs of hers that would have effectively prevented James asking further favours. It had no effect on Mirabel.

'Just this once. After tomorrow I'll stay at home like a good little mum and in a month Mrs Hodges will be back. Just from seven till — well, eleven would be the absolute latest.'

'I'll sit with Oliver,' said James's mother.

Mirabel's guarantee came to nothing, however, for far from staying home with Oliver, she turned up at Ewes Hall Farm three days later, this time to leave him with them while she went shopping with Gilbert's mother. She was gone for four hours. Oliver made himself sick from eating toffees he found in Rosamund's room and he had uprooted six houseplants and stripped off their leaves before James caught him at it.

Next time, James's mother said she would put her foot down. She had already promised to sit with Oliver on the coming Saturday night. That she would do and that must be the end of it. And this resolve was strengthened by Mirabel's failure to return home until half-past one on the Sunday morning. She would have told Mirabel so in no uncertain terms, Elizabeth Fyfield told her family at breakfast, but Gilbert Coleridge had been there and she had not wanted to embarrass Mirabel in front of him.

On the Tuesday, the day to which the Women's Institute meeting had been put forward, the fine weather broke with a storm which gave place by the afternoon to steady rain. James was spending the day turning out the glory-hole. He had been told to do it often enough and he had meant to do it, but who would be indoors in a stuffy bedroom when the sun is shining and the temperature in the eighties? That Tuesday was a very suitable sort of day for disposing of books one had outgrown, tanks and cages and jars that were no longer inhabited, for throwing away collections that had become just boxfuls of rubbish, for making a clean sweep on the path to adulthood.

Taking down the books from the top shelf, he came upon an object whose existence he had almost forgotten — the bottle labelled *datura stramonium*. That was something he need not hesitate to throw away. He looked at it curiously, at the clear greenish-brown fluid it contained and which seemed in the past months to have settled and clarified. Why had he made it and what for? In another age, he thought he might have been an alchemist or a warlock, and he shook his head ruefully at the juvenile James who was no more.

So many of these books held no interest for him any longer. They were kids' stuff. He began stacking them in a 'wanted' and an 'unwanted' pile on the floor. Palmerston sat on the window sill and watched him, unblinking golden eyes in a big round grey face. It was a good thing, James thought, that he had ceased keeping mice before Palmerston arrived. Perhaps the mouse cage could be sold. There was someone in his class at school who kept hamsters and had been talking of getting an extra cage. It wouldn't do any harm to give him a ring.

James went down to the living room and picked up the receiver to dial Timothy Gordon's number; the phone was dead. There was no dialling tone but a silence broken by occasional faint clicks and crepitations. He would have to go up the lane to the call box and phone the engineers, but not now, later. It was pouring with rain.

As he was crossing the hall and was almost at the foot of the stairs the doorbell rang. His mother had said something about the laundry coming. James opened the door absent-mindedly, prepared to nod to the man and take in the laundry box, and saw instead Mirabel.

Her car was parked on the drive and staring out of its front window was Oliver, chewing something, his fingers plastering the glass with stickiness. Mirabel was dressed up to the nines, as Aunt Julie might have said, and dressed very unsuitably for the weather in a trailing, cream-coloured pleated affair with beads round her neck and two or three chiffon scarves and pale pink stockings and cream shoes that were all straps no thicker than bits of string.

'Oh, James, you are going to be an angel, aren't you, and have Oliver for me just for the afternoon? You won't be on your own, Rosamund's in, I saw her looking out of her bedroom window. I did try to ring you but your phone's out of order.'

Mirabel said this in an accusing tone as if James had purposely broken the phone himself. She was rather breathless and seemed in a hurry.

'Why can't you take him with you?' said James.

'Because, if you must know, Gilbert is going to buy me

something rather special and important and I can't take a baby along.'

Rosamund, under the impression that excitement was afoot, appeared at the bend in the staircase.

'It's only Mirabel,' said James.

But Mirabel took the opportunity, while his attention was distracted, of rushing to the car — her finery getting much spotted with rain in the process — and seizing the sticky Oliver.

'You'd like to stay with James and Rosamund, wouldn't you, sweetheart?'

'Do we have to?' said Rosamund, coming downstairs and bestowing on Oliver a look of such unmistakeable distaste that even Mirabel flinched. Flinched but didn't give up. Indeed, she thrust Oliver at James, keeping his sticky mouth well clear of her dress, and James had no choice but to grab hold of him. Oliver immediately started to whine and hold out his arms to his mother.

'No, darling, you'll see Mummy later. Now listen, James. Mrs Hodges's daughter is going to come for him at five-thirty. That's when she finishes work. She's going to take him back to her place and I'll pick him up when I get home. And now I must fly, I'm meeting Gilbert at three.'

'Well!' exploded Rosamund as the car disappeared down the drive.

'Isn't she the end? Fancy getting lumbered with *him*. I was going to do my holiday art project.'

'I was going to turn my room out, but it's no good moaning. We've got him and that's that.'

Oliver, once the front door was closed, had begun to whimper.

'If it wasn't raining we could go in the garden. We could take him out for a walk.'

'It *is* raining,' said James. 'And what would we take him in? Mum's basket on wheels? The wheelbarrow? In case you hadn't noticed, dear Mirabel didn't think to bring his push chair. Come on, let's take him in the kitchen. The best thing to do with him is to feed him. He shuts up when he's eating.'

In the larder James found a packet of Penguin biscuits, the chocolate-covered kind, and gave one to Oliver. Oliver sat on the floor and ate it, throwing down little bits of red and gold wrapping paper. Then he opened the saucepan cupboard and began taking out all the pots and pans and the colander and the sieves, getting chocolate all over the white Melamine finish on the door. Rosamund wiped the door and then she wiped him which made him grizzle and hit out at her with his fists. When the saucepans were spread about the floor, Oliver opened all the drawers one after the other and took out cutlery and cheese graters and potato peelers and dishcloths and dusters.

James watched him gloomily. 'I read somewhere that a child of two, even a child with a very high IQ, can't ever concentrate on one thing for more than nineteen minutes at a time.'

'And Oliver isn't two yet and I don't think his IQ's all that amazing.'

'Exactly,' said James.

'Ink,' said Oliver. He kicked the knives and forks out of his way and came to James, hitting out with a wooden spoon. 'Ink.'

'Imagine him with ink,' said Rosamund.

'He's probably not saying ink. It's something else he means only we don't know what.'

'Ink, ink, ink!'

'If we lived in London we could take him for a ride on a bus. We could take him to the zoo.'

'If we lived in London,' said James, 'we wouldn't be looking after him. I tell you what, I reckon he'd like television. Mirabel hasn't got television.'

He picked Oliver up and carried him into the living room. The furniture in there was dark brown leather and would not

mark so it seemed sensible to give him another Penguin.
James switched the television on. At this time of day there
wasn't much on of interest to anyone, let alone someone of
Oliver's age, only a serial about people working at an airport. Oliver, however, seemed entranced by the colours and
the movement, so James shoved him into the back of an
armchair and with a considerable feeling of relief left him.

There was a good deal of clearing up to be done in the
kitchen. Oliver had got brown stains on two tablecloths and
James had to wash the knives and forks. Rosamund (typi-
cally, he thought) had vanished. Back to her art project, presumably, making some sort of collage with dried flowers.
He put all the saucepans back and tidied up the drawers so
that they looked much as they had done before Oliver's on-
slaught. Then he thought he had better go back and see how
Oliver was getting on.

The living room was empty. James could soon see why.
The serial had come to an end and the bright moving figures
and voices and music had been replaced by an old man with
glasses talking about molecular physics. Oliver wasn't anywhere downstairs. James hadn't really imagined he could
climb stairs, but of course he could. He was a big strong boy
who had been walking for months and months now.

He went up, calling Oliver's name. It was only a quarter
past three and his mother wouldn't be back from the village
hall until four-thirty at the earliest. The rain was coming
down harder now, making the house rather dark. James realized for the first time that he had left his bedroom door open.
He had left it open — because Palmerston was inside —
when he went downstairs to phone Timothy Gordon about
the mouse cage, and then Mirabel had come. It all seemed
hours ago but it was only about forty minutes.

Oliver was in James's bedroom. He was sitting on the
floor with the empty *datura* bottle clutched in his hands, and
from the side of the mouth trickled a dribble of brown fluid.

James had read in books about people being rooted to the

spot and that was exactly what happened at that moment. He seemed anchored where he stood. He stared at Oliver. In his inside there seemed to swell up and throb a large hard lump. It was his own heart beating so heavily that it hurt.

He forced himself to move. He took the bottle away from Oliver and automatically, he didn't know why, rinsed it out in silence. James went down the passage and banged on Rosamund's door.

'Could you come, please? Oliver's drunk a bottle of poison. About half a pint.'

'*What?*' She came out. She looked at him, her mouth open. He explained to her swiftly, shortly, in two sentences.

'What are we going to do?'

'Phone for an ambulance.'

She stood in the bedroom doorway, watching Oliver. He had put his fists in his eyes, he was rubbing his eyes and making fretful little sounds.

'D'you think we ought to try and make him sick?'

'No. I'll go and phone. It's my fault. I must have been out of my tree making the stuff, let alone keeping it. If he dies. . . Oh, God, Roz, we can't phone! The phone's out of order. I was trying to phone Tim Gordon but it was dead and I was going to go down to the call box and report it.'

'You can go to the call box now.'

'That means you'll have to stay with him.'

Rosamund's lip quivered. She looked at the little boy who was lying on the floor now, his eyes wide open, his thumb in his mouth. 'I don't want to. Suppose he dies?'

'You go,' said James. 'I'll stay with him. Go to the call box and dial nine-nine-nine for an ambulance and then go into the village hall and fetch mum, OK?'

'OK,' said Rosamund, and she went, the tears running down her face.

James picked Oliver up and laid him gently on the bed. There were beads of perspiration on the child's face but that might have been simply because he was hot. Mirabel had wrapped him very warmly for the time of the year in a woolly cardigan as well as a jumper and a tee-shirt. He had been thirsty, of course. That was what 'ink' had meant. 'Ink' for 'drink'. Was there the slightest chance that during the year since he had made it the *datura* had lost its toxicity? He did not honestly think so. He could remember reading somewhere that the poison was resistant to drying and to heat, so probably it was also resistant to time.

Oliver's eyes were closed now and some of the bright red colour which had been in his face while he was watching television had faded. His fat cheeks looked waxen. At any rate, he didn't seem to be in pain, though the sweat stood in tiny glistening pinpoints on his forehead. James asked himself again why he had been such a fool as to keep the stuff. An hour before he had been on the point of throwing it away and yet he had not. It was useless to have regrets, to 'job backwards', as his father put it.

But James was looking to the future, not to the past. Suddenly he knew that if Oliver died he would have murdered him as surely, or almost as surely, as if he had fired at him with his father's shotgun. And his whole life, his entire future, would be wrecked. For he would never forgive himself, never recover, never be anything but a broken person. He would have to hide away, live in a distant part of the country, go to a different school, and when he left that school get some obscure job and drag out a frightened, haunted existence. Gone would be his dreams of Oxford, of work in some research establishment, of happiness and fulfilment and success. He was not overdramatizing, he knew it would be so. And Mirabel. . . ? If his life would be in ruins, what of hers?

He heard the front door open and his mother come running up the stairs. He was sitting on the bed, watching Oliver, and he turned round slowly.

'Oh, James. . .!'

And James said like a mature man, like a man three times

his age, 'There's nothing you can say to me I haven't already said to myself.'

She touched his shoulder. 'I know that,' she said. 'I know you.' Her face was white, the lips too, and with anger as much as fear. 'How dare she bring him here and leave him with two *children*?'

James hadn't the spirit to feel offended. 'Is he — is he *dying*?'

'He's asleep,' said his mother and she put her hand on Oliver's head. It was quite cool, the sweat had dried. 'At least, I suppose he is. He could be in a coma, for all I know.'

'It will be the end of me if he dies.'

'James, oh, James. . .' She did something she had not done for a long time. She put her arms round him and held him close to her, though he was half a head taller than she.

Two men came up the stairs for Oliver. One of them wrapped him in a blanket and carried him downstairs in his arms. Rosamund was sitting in the hall with Palmerston on her lap and she was crying silently into his fur. It seemed hard to leave her but someone had to wait in for Mrs Hodges's daughter. James and his mother got into the ambulance with Oliver and went with him to the hospital.

They had to sit in a waiting room while the doctors did things to Oliver — pumped his stomach, presumably. Then a young black doctor and an old white doctor came and asked James a whole string of questions. What exactly was the stuff Oliver had drunk? When was it made? How much of it had been in the bottle? And a host of others. They were not pleasant to him and he wanted to prevaricate. It would be so easy to say he hadn't known what the stuff really was, that he had boiled the thornapples up to make a green dye, or something like that. But when it came to it he couldn't. He had to tell the bald truth, he had to say he had made poison, knowing it might kill.

After they had gone away there was a long wait in which nothing happened. Mrs Hodges's daughter would have come by now and James's father would be home from where he was teaching at a summer seminar. It got to five-thirty, to six, when a nurse brought them a cup of tea, and then there was another long wait. James thought that no matter what happened to him in years to come, nothing could actually be worse than those hours in the waiting room had been. Just before seven the young doctor came back. He seemed to think James's mother was Oliver's mother and when he realized she was not he just shrugged and said as if they couldn't be all that anxious, as if it wouldn't be a matter of great importance to them:

'He'll be O.K. No need for you to hang about any longer.'

James's mother jumped to her feet with a little cry. 'He's all right? He's really all right?'

'Perfectly, as far as we can tell. The stomach contents are being analysed. We'll keep him in for tonight, though, just to be on the safe side.'

The Fyfield family all sat up to wait for Mirabel. They were going to wait up, no matter what time she came, even if she didn't come till two in the morning. A note, put into the letter box of Sindon Lodge, warned her what had happened and told her to phone the hospital.

James was bracing himself for a scene. On the way back from the hospital his mother had told him he must be prepared for Mirabel to say some very unpleasant things to him. Women who would foist their children on to anyone and often seemed indifferent to them were usually most likely to become hysterical when those children were in danger. It was guilt, she supposed. But James thought that if Mirabel raved she had a right to, for although Oliver had not died and would not, he might easily have done. He was only alive because they had been very quick about getting that deadly stuff out of him. Mirabel wouldn't be able to phone Ewes Hall Farm, for the phone was still out of order. They all had coffee at about ten and James's father, who had gone all over his room to make sure there were no more killing bottles and had given James a stern but just lecture on responsibility, poured himself a large whiskey.

The yellow Volvo came up the drive at twenty to twelve. James sat tight and kept calm the way he had resolved to do while his father went to answer the door. He waited to hear a shriek or a sob. Rosamund had put her fingers in her ears.

The front door closed and there were footsteps. Mirabel walked in, smiling. She had a big diamond on the third finger of her left hand. James's mother got up and went to her, holding out her hands, looking into Mirabel's face.

'You found our note? Of course you must have. Mirabel, I hardly know what to say to you. . .'

Before Mirabel could say anything James's father came in with the man she was going to marry, a big teddy bear of a man with a handlebar moustache. James found himself shaking hands. It was all very different from what he had expected. And Mirabel was all smiles, vague and happy, showing off her engagement ring on her thin little hand.

'What did they say when you phoned the hospital?'

'I didn't.'

'You didn't phone? But surely you. . . ?'

'I knew he was all right, Elizabeth. I didn't want to make a fool of myself telling them he'd drunk half a pint of coloured water, did I?'

James stared at her. And suddenly her gaiety fell from her as she realized what she had said. Her hand went up to cover her mouth and a dark flush mottled her face. She stepped back and took Gilbert Coleridge's arm.

'I'm afraid you underrate my son's abilities as a toxicologist,' said James's father, and Mirabel took her hand down and made a serious face and said that of course they must get back so that she could phone at once.

James knew then. He understood. The room seemed to move round him in a slow circle and to rock up and down. He knew what Mirabel had done, and although it would not be the end of him or ruin things for him or spoil his future, it would be with him all his life. And in Mirabel's eyes he saw that she knew he knew.

But they were moving back towards the hall now in a flurry of excuses and thank yous and good nights, and the room had settled back into its normal shape and equilibrium. James said to Mirabel, and his voice had a break in it for the first time: 'Good night, I'm sorry I was so stupid.'

She would understand what he meant.

May and June

Their parents named them May and June because their birthdays occurred in those months. A third sister, an April child, had been christened Avril but she had died. May was like the time of year in which she had been born, changeable, chilly and warm by turns, sullen yet able to know and show a loveliness that couldn't last.

In the nineteen thirties, when May was in her twenties, it was still important to get one's daughters well married, and though Mrs Thrace had no anxieties on that head for sunny June, she was less sanguine with regard to May. Her elder daughter was neither pretty nor graceful nor clever, and no man had ever looked at her twice. June, of course, had a string of admirers. Then May met a young lawyer at a *thé dansant*. His name was Walter Symonds, he was extremely good looking, his father was wealthy and made him a generous allowance, and there was no doubt he belonged in a higher social class than that of the Thraces. May fell passionately in love with him, but no one was more surprised than she when he asked her to marry him.

The intensity of her passion frightened Mrs Thrace. It

wasn't quite nice. The expression on her face while she awaited the coming of her fiancé, her ardour when she greeted him, the hunger in her eyes — that sort of thing was all very well in the cinema, but unsuitable for a civil servant's daughter in a genteel suburb.

Briefly, she had become almost beautiful. 'I'm going to marry him,' she said when warned. 'He wants me to love him, doesn't he? He loves me. Why shouldn't I show my love?'

June, who was clever as well as pretty, was away at college training to be a schoolteacher. It had been considered wiser, long before Walter Symonds was thought of, to keep May at home. She had no particular aptitude for anything and she was useful to her mother about the house. Now, of course, it turned out that she had an aptitude for catching a rich, handsome and successful husband. Then, a month before the wedding, June came home for the summer holidays.

It was all very unfortunate, Mrs Thrace said over and over again. If Walter Symonds had jilted May for some unknown girl, they would have been bitterly indignant, enraged even, and Mr Thrace would have felt old-fashioned longings to apply a horsewhip. But what could anyone say or do when he transferred his affections from the elder daughter to the younger?

May screamed and sobbed and tried to attack June with a knife. 'We're all terribly sorry for you, my darling,' said Mrs Thrace, 'but what can anyone do? You wouldn't marry a man who doesn't love you, would you?'

'He does love me, he does! It's just because she's pretty. She's cast a spell on him. I wish she was dead and then he'd love me again.'

'You mustn't say that, May. It's all very cruel, but you have to face the fact that he's changed his mind. Isn't it better to find out now than later?'

'I would have had him,' said May.

Mrs Thrace blushed. She was shocked to the core.

'I shall never marry now,' said May. 'She's ruined my life and I shall never have anything ever again.'

Walter and June were married, and Walter's father bought them a big house in Surrey. May stayed at home, being useful to her mother. The war came. Walter went straight into the army, became a captain, a major, finally a colonel. May also went into the army, where she remained a private for five years, working in some catering department. After that, there was nothing for it but to go home to her parents once more.

She never forgave her sister.

'She stole my husband,' she said to her mother.

'He wasn't your husband, May.'

'As good as. You wouldn't forgive a thief who came into your house and stole the most precious thing you had or were likely to have.'

'We're told to forgive those who trespass against us, as we hope to be forgiven.'

'I'm not religious,' said May, and on those occasions when the Symondses came to the Thrace home she took care to be out of it. But she knew all about them — all, that is, except one thing.

Mr and Mrs Thrace were most careful never to speak of June in her presence, so May listened outside the door, and she secretly read all June's letters to her mother. Whenever Walter's name was spoken or mentioned in a letter, she winced and shivered with the pain of it. She knew that they had moved to a much larger house, that they were building up a collection of furniture and pictures. She knew where they went for their holidays and what friends they entertained. But what she was never able to discover was how Walter felt about June. Had he ever really loved her? Had he repented of his choice? May thought that perhaps, after the first flush of infatuation was over, he had come to long for his former love as much as she longed for him. Since she never saw them she could never know, for, however he might feel, Walter couldn't leave June. When you have done what he had done you can't change again. You have to stick it out till death.

It comforted her, it was perhaps the only thing that kept her going, to convince herself that Walter regretted his bargain. If there had been children, what the Victorians called pledges of love. . .

Sometimes, after a letter had come from June, May would see her mother looked particularly pleased and satisfied. And then, shaking with dread, she would read the letter, terrified to find that June was pregnant. But Mrs Thrace's pleasure and satisfaction must have come from some other source, from some account of Walter's latest coup in court or June's latest party, for no children came and now June was past forty.

Trained for nothing, May worked as canteen supervisor in a women's hostel. She continued to live at home until her parents died. Their deaths took place within six months, Mrs Thrace dying in March and her widower in August. And that was how it happened that May saw Walter again.

At the time of her mother's cremation, May was ill with a virus infection and unable to attend. But she had no way of avoiding her father's funeral. When she saw Walter come into the church a faintness seized her and she huddled against the pew rail, trembling. She covered her face with her hands to make it seem as if she were praying, and when at last she took them away he was beside her. He took her hand and looked into her face. May's eyes met his which were as blue and compelling as ever, and she saw with anguish that he had lost none of his looks but that they had become only more distinguished. She would have liked to die then, holding his hand and gazing into his face.

'Won't you come and speak to your sister, May?' said Walter in the rich deep voice which charmed juries, struck terror into the hearts of witnesses and won women. 'Shall we let bygones be bygones on this very sad day?'

May shivered. She withdrew her hand and marched to the back of the church. She placed herself as far away from June as she could get, but not too far to observe that it was June who took Walter's arm as they left and not Walter June's, June who looked up to Walter for comfort while his face remained grave and still, June who clung to him while he merely permitted the clinging. It couldn't be that he was behaving like that because she, May, was there. He must hate and despise June as she, with all her heart, hated and despised her still.

But it was at a funeral that they were reconciled. May learnt of Walter's death through reading an announcement of it in a newspaper. And the pain of it was as great as that she had suffered when her mother had told her he wanted to marry June. She sent flowers, an enormous wreath of snow-white roses that cost her half a week's wages. And of course she would go to the funeral, whether June wanted her there or not.

Apparently June did want her. Perhaps she thought the roses were for the living bereaved and not for the dead. She came up to May and put her arms round her, laying her head against her sister's shoulder in misery and despair. May broke their long silence.

'Now you know what it's like to lose him,' she said.

'Oh, May, May, don't be cruel to me now! Don't hold that against me now. Be kind to me now. I've nothing left.'

So May sat beside June, and after the funeral she went back to the house where June had lived with Walter. In saying she had nothing left, June had presumably been referring to emotional rather than material goods. Apart from certain stately homes she had visited on tours, May had never seen anything like the interior of that house.

'I'm going to retire next month,' she said, 'and then I'll be living in what they call a flatlet — one room and a kitchen.'

Two days later there came a letter from June.

'Dearest May, Don't be angry with me for calling you
that. You have always been one of my dearest, in spite of
what I did and in spite of your hatred of me. I can't be sorry
for what I did because so much happiness came of it for me,
but I am truly, deeply, sorry that you were the one to suffer.
And now, dear May, I want to try to make up to you for
what I did, though I know I can never really do that, not
now, not after so long. You said you were going to retire and
wouldn't be living very comfortably. Will you come and
live with me? You can have as many rooms in this house as
you want, you are welcome to share everything with me.
You will know what I mean when I say I feel that would be
just. Please make me happy by saying you forgive me and
will come. Always your loving sister, June.'

What did the trick was June saying it would be just. Yes,
it would be justice if May could now have some of those
good things which were hers by right and which June had
stolen from her along with her man. She waited a week before replying and then she wrote: 'Dear June, What you suggest seems a good idea. I have thought about it and I will
make my home with you. I have very little personal property, so moving will not be a great headache. Let me know
when you want me to come. It is raining again here and very
cold. Yours, May.' There was nothing, however, in the letter about forgiveness.

And yet May, sharing June's house, was almost prepared
to forgive. For she was learning at last what June's married
life had been.

'You can talk about him if you want to,' she had said hungrily on their first evening together. 'If it's going to relieve
your feelings, I don't mind.'

'What is there to say except that we were married for forty
years and now he's dead?'

'You could show me some of the things he gave you.'
May picked up ornaments, gazed at pictures. 'Did he give
you that? What about this?'

'They weren't presents. I bought them or he did.'

May couldn't help getting excited. 'I wonder you're not afraid of burglars. This is a proper Aladdin's Cave. Have you got lots of jewellery too?'

'Not much,' said June uncomfortably.

May's eyes were on June's engagement ring, a poor thing of diamond chips in nine carat gold, far less expensive than the ring Walter had given his first love. Of course she had kept hers and Walter, though well off even then, hadn't been rich enough to buy a second magnificent ring within six months of the first. But later, surely. . . ?

'I should have thought you'd have an eternity ring.'

'Marriage doesn't last for eternity,' said June. 'Let's not talk about it any more.'

May could tell she didn't like talking about it. Soon she shied at mentioning Walter's name and she put away the photographs of him which had stood on the piano and the drawing room mantelpiece. May wondered if Walter had ever written any letters to his wife. They had seldom been parted, of course, but it would be strange if June had received no letter from him in forty years. The first time June went out alone, May tried to open her desk. It was locked. The drawers of June's dressing table disclosed a couple of birthday cards with 'Love from Walter' scrawled hastily on them, and the only other written message from her husband June had considered worth keeping May found tucked into a cookery book in the kitchen. It was a note written on the back of a bill, and it read: 'Baker called. I ordered large white for Saturday.'

That night May reread the two letters she had received from Walter during their engagement. Each began, 'Dearest May.' She hadn't looked at them for forty years — she hadn't dared — but now she read them with calm satisfaction. 'Dearest May, This is the first love letter I have ever written. If it isn't much good you must put it down to lack of practice. I miss you a lot and rather wish I hadn't told my parents I would come on this holiday with them. . .' 'Dearest May, Thanks for both your letters. Sorry I've taken so long to reply but I feel a bit nervous that my letters don't match up to yours. Still, with luck, we soon shan't have to write to each other because we shan't be separated. I wish you were here with me. . .' Poor Walter had been reticent and shy, unable to express his feelings on paper or by word of mouth. But at least he had written love letters to her and not notes about loaves of bread. May decided to start wearing her engagement ring again — on her little finger of course because she could no longer get it over the knuckles of her ring finger. If June noticed she didn't remark on it.

'Was it you or Walter who didn't want children?' May asked.

'Children just didn't come.'

'Walter *must* have wanted them. When he was engaged to me we talked of having three.'

June looked upset but May could have talked of Walter all day long.

'He was only sixty-five,' she said. 'That's young to die these days. You never told me what he died of.'

'Cancer,' said June. 'They operated but he never regained consciousness.'

'Just like mother,' said May. Suppose June had had cancer and had died, what would have happened then? Remembering Walter's tender look and strong handclasp at her father's funeral, May thought he would have married her. She twisted the ring on her little finger. 'You were almost like a second wife, weren't you? It must be a difficult position.'

'I'd much rather not talk about it,' said June, and with her handkerchief to her eyes she left the room.

May was happy. For the first time in forty years she was happy. She busied herself about the house, caring for June's things, dusting and polishing, pausing to look at a picture and reflecting that Walter must often have looked at it. Sometimes she imagined him sitting in this chair or standing

by that window, his heart full of regret for what he might
have had. And she thought now, while he had been longing
for her she, far away, had been crying for him. She never
cried now, though June did.

'I'm an old fool, I can't help giving way. You're strong,
May, but I'm weak and I miss him so.'

'Didn't I miss him?'

'He was always fond of you. It upset him a lot to think
you were unhappy. He often talked about you.' June looked
at her piteously. 'You have forgiven me, haven't you,
May?'

'As a matter of fact, I have,' said May. She was a little
surprised at herself but, yes, she had forgiven June. 'I think
you've been punished for what you did.' A loveless marriage, a husband who talked constantly of another
woman. . .

'I've been punished,' said June and she put her arms
round May's neck.

The strong and the weak, May remembered those words
when a movement downstairs woke her in the night. She
heard footsteps and the sound of a door being forced. It was
the burglar she feared and had warned June about, but June
would be cowering in her room now, incapable of taking
any action.

May put on her dressing gown and went stealthily along
the passage to June's room. The bed was empty. She looked
out of the window, and the moonlight showed her a car
parked on the gravel drive that led down to the lane. A
yellower, stronger light streamed from the drawing room
window. A shiver of fear went through her, but she knew
she must be strong.

Before she reached the head of the stairs she heard a violent crash as of something heavy yet brittle hurled against a
wall. There was a cry from below, footsteps running. May
got to the stairs in time to see a slight figure rush across the
hall and slam the front door behind him. The car started up.

In his wake he had left a thin trail of blood. May followed the blood trail into the drawing room. June stood by her desk which had been torn open and all its contents scattered on to the table. She was trembling, tearful and laughing with shaky hysteria, pointing to the shards of cut glass that lay everywhere.

'I threw the decanter at him. I hit him and it cut his head and he ran.'

May went up to her. 'Are you all right?'

'He didn't touch me. He pointed that gun at me when I came in, but I didn't care. I couldn't bear to see him searching my desk, getting at all my private things. Wasn't I brave? He didn't get away with anything but a few bits of silver. I hit him and he heard you coming and he panicked. Wasn't I brave, May?'

But May wasn't listening. She was reading the letter which lay open and exposed on top of the paper the burglar had pulled out of the desk. Walter's bold handwriting leapt at her, weakened though it was, enfeebled by his last illness. 'My darling love, it is only a moment since you walked out of the ward, but nevertheless I must write to you. I can't resist an impulse to write now and tell you how happy you have made me in all the years we have been together. If the worst comes to the worst, my darling, and I don't survive the operation, I want you to know you are the only woman I ever loved. . .'

'I wouldn't have thought I'd have had the courage,' said June, 'but perhaps the gun wasn't loaded. He was only a boy. Would you call the police, please, May?'

'Yes,' said May. She picked up the gun.

The police arrived within fifteen minutes. They brought a doctor with them, but June was already dead, shot through the heart at close range.

'We'll get him, Miss Thrace, don't you worry,' said the inspector.

'It was a pity you touched the gun, though. Did it without thinking, I suppose?'

'It was the shock,' said May. 'I've never had a shock like that, not since I was a girl.'

A Needle for
the Devil

The devil finds work for idle hands to do, as Mrs Gibson used to say to her daughter, and Alice had found that in her case the devil (or her own mysterious inner compulsions) led her to violence. As a child she would strike people who annoyed her and when she was fourteen she attacked her sister with a knife, though no harm was done. But if her hands itched to injure, they were also gifted hands and as she was taught to occupy them with handicrafts, the impulse to violence grew less. Or was sublimated, as she learned to say when she began training to be a nurse.

Only her mother had opposed Alice's choice of a career. Perhaps it was only her mother who understood her. But her objections were overruled by Alice's father, her headmistress, the school careers officer and Alice herself. And certainly Alice did well. There were no unfortunate incidents of the kind Mrs Gibson had feared.

Naturally, in her new life, she had had to abandon her handicrafts. One cannot keep a loom or a potter's wheel in one's room in the nurses' residence. And there were many occasions when Alice would come off duty worn-out, not so much from lifting patients, making beds and running to and fro, as from the exercise of an iron self-control. The impulse to hit, pinch or otherwise manhandle a patient who had angered her had to be constantly suppressed.

Then the girl who shared her room came back from two days off duty wearing a knee-length white wool coat.

'I love your coat,' said Alice. 'It's gorgeous. It must have cost the earth.'

'I made it,' said Pamela.

'You *made* it? You mean you knitted it?'

'It wasn't very difficult and it only took three weeks.'

Alice had never thought of knitting. Knitting was something one's grandmother did or one's aunts or pregnant women making layettes. But if Pamela could make the coat, which neither savoured of aunts nor was layette-like, she was very sure she could. And it might solve that problem of hers which had lately become so pressing that she was afraid she might have to leave without finishing her training.

Knitting has the advantage over sewing or weaving that it requires basically only a ball of wool and a pair of needles. It can be done in one's lunch break, in a train, during night duty. It calms the nerves, occupies the hands, provides therapy — and supplies a wardrobe. Alice began knitting with enthusiasm and found that, because of its ubiquity and the way it can be taken up at any free moment, it answered her purpose better than any of her other crafts had done.

She progressed in her career, became a staff nurse, a sister, and by the time she was thirty had full charge of the men's medical ward at St Gregory's Hospital for Officers. It was there, three or four years later, that she first set eyes on Rupert Clarigate who had been brought in after having a heart attack.

Rupert Clarigate was fifty-two at the time of his coronary. He was a bachelor who had retired from the army two years before with the rank of Lieutenant Colonel and had since been living very comfortably — too comfortably perhaps —

on his handsome pension. Had he smoked less and walked more, eaten less lavishly of roast pheasant at his club and drunk less old Napoleon brandy afterwards he might not, according to his doctor, have been seized one night by a fierce pain down his left arm and up his left side and found himself a moment later lying on the floor, fighting for breath. His doctor was one of those who believe that a coronary patient should never be left unattended for the first few days after an attack. Hence, St Gregory's and Sister Gibson. On his first morning in hospital he awoke to look into the sea-blue eyes of a slim young woman in a trim uniform whose blonde hair was half-covered by a starched white coif.

'Good morning, Colonel Clarigate,' said Alice. 'My goodness, but aren't you looking better this morning! It just shows what a good night's sleep can do.'

Alice said this sort of thing to all her new patients but Rupert, who had never been in hospital before and had in fact been riotously healthy all his life till now, thought it was specially designed for him and that her tone was exceptionally sweet. He did not hear her, five minutes later, telling one of her students who had dropped a kidney dish that she was not only hopelessly unfitted to be a nurse but mentally retarded as well, because this diatribe was delivered in the cleansing department off the ward known as the sluice. He thought Alice must have a delightful disposition, always cheerful, always encouraging, endlessly patient, as well as being the sort of girl who looked as if she knew how to have a good time.

'Who's the lucky chap that's taking you out tonight, sister?' Rupert said as Alice put her head round the door before going off duty. 'I envy him, I don't mind telling you.'

'No chap, Colonel,' said Alice. 'I'm going to have a quiet evening doing my knitting in front of the TV.'

Those statements were quite true. There was no chap. There had been in days gone by, several in fact, including one whom Alice would probably have married had she not once slapped his face (and thereby dislodged a filling from a molar) for teasing her. But she had been very young then and without her prop and resort. Since those days she had put her career before a possible husband and had become so used to the overtures and the flirtatious remarks of patients that she hardly took in what they said and scarcely thought of them as men.

Rupert Clarigate, however, was different. He was one of the handsomest men she had ever seen and he had such a wonderful head of hair. For although his face was still youthful and unlined, his hair was snow-white; white and thick and ever so slightly wavy, and since he had left the army it had been allowed to grow just long enough to cover the tops of his ears. It was the first thing Alice had noticed about him. She had always felt a peculiar antipathy to baldness, and though accustomed to the most repulsive sights and to washing a wound or cleaning an abscess without a flicker of distaste, it was still as much as she could do to wash a man's bald pate or comb the hair which surrounded it. Rupert Clarigate looked as if he would never be bald, for not even a coin-sized bare spot showed amid the lush snowy mass.

Besides that, she liked his hearty jovial manner, the public school accent, the Sandhurst voice. The slightly lecherous admiration in his eyes, kept well under control, excited her. By the end of the first week of his stay she was in love, or would have said she was in love, having no criterion to judge by.

As for Colonel Clarigate, he had always intended to get married one day. A long-standing affair with another officer's wife had kept him single till he was thirty-five and after that was over he felt too set in his ways to embark on matrimony. Too selfish, the other officer's wife said. And it was true that Rupert could see no point in having a wife when he didn't want to stay in in the evenings, had no desire for children, disliked the idea of sharing his income and in any case had his officer's servant to wait on him and clean his quarters.

But he would marry one day — when he retired. Now retirement had come and he was living in the big inconvenient old house his parents had left him. There was no one to keep it clean. He ate rich food in expensive restaurants because there was no one at home to cook for him and he told himself he smoked too much because he was lonely. In fact, he had had his heart attack because he had no wife. Why should not pretty, efficient, kindly Sister Gibson be his wife?

Why not retire from nursing? thought Alice. Why should she not marry Colonel Clarigate and have a home of her own instead of a two-room flat that went with the job? Besides, she was in love with him and he had such beautiful thick hair.

He must be in love with Sister Gibson, thought Rupert, otherwise he would surely not feel so uneasy about her in the evenings when he was certain she must be out with some chap. This, he knew from his experience with the other officer's wife, was jealousy and a proof of love.

He left the hospital after three weeks and went to convalesce in the country. From there he wrote to Alice nearly every day. When he came home again he took her to the theatre to see a slapstick sexy comedy at which they both laughed very much, and then to the cinema to see a reissue of *Carry On Nurse* which had them equally convulsed. On their third evening out together they became engaged.

'People may say it was sudden,' said Alice, 'but I feel we know each other through and through. After all there's no more intimate situation, is there, than that of nurse and patient?'

'I can think of one,' said Rupert with a wink, and they both fell about laughing.

His fifty-third birthday occurred about a month after their engagement and Alice knitted him a pullover. It was rust red, bordered at the welt and on the neckline with fine stripes of cream and dark green and it suited him well, for Rupert, in spite of his high living, had never become fat. Alice insisted on looking after him. She took him out for sensible walks and gently discouraged him from smoking. The Clarigate house was not to her taste so he set about selling it and buying another. The prospect of furnishing this house which was in a seaside resort on the south coast — they could live anywhere they chose, Rupert said, there was no need to stay in London — filled Alice with excited anticipation, especially as Rupert was giving her a free hand with his savings.

The marriage took place in May, three months after their first meeting.

It was a quiet wedding, followed by a small luncheon party Mrs Gibson, now a widow, was present and so was Alice's sister and that friend Pamela who had introduced her to the charms of knitting, and Pamela's husband Guy, a freelance writer and author of mystery novels. On Rupert's side were a cousin of his and his former commanding officer and Dr Nicholson, that conscientious medical man who had been responsible for sending him to St Gregory's. The newly married couple left at three to catch the plane that was to take them to Barbados for their honeymoon.

Alice had never before been away on a holiday without taking her knitting with her. In Palma de Mallorca she had knitted a Fair Isle cap and gloves for her niece, in Innsbruck she had begun an Aran for her brother-in-law and in the Isles of Greece she had finished a slipover for herself. But some instinct as to the rightness or suitability of certain actions told her that one does not take knitting on one's honeymoon, and indeed she found there would scarcely have been the opportunity to knit. One can hardly knit on a beach and they were mostly on the beach when they were not dining and dancing, for Rupert had been right when he assessed his wife as a girl who knew how to have a good time. Alice would have danced harder, eaten more heartily and stayed up even later were it not for her prudent care of her husband's health. While Rupert, vigorous and virile as he was, might in some ways seem as young as she, there was no getting away from the fact that he had had one coronary and might have another. She was glad to see that he had given up smoking and if, towards the end of their stay, she noticed an edge to his temper, she put this down to the heat.

Furnishing the new house took up all her time once they were returned. There were carpets to choose and order, plumbing and heating and electrical engineers to call, upholsterers and curtain makers to be urged on. Alice worked briskly, refusing to allow Rupert to help, but taking him out each evening with her for a therapeutic stroll along the sea front. He looked fitter than he had in all the five months she had known him and he could run upstairs now without shortness of breath.

It was on the morning after the day when the new carpets were fitted, after Alice had rearranged and polished the furniture, that she felt she could at last begin to relax. Rupert had gone to Dr Nicholson's for his monthly check-up. She set out for the shopping centre to buy herself some wool. On the previous evening, while they were out for their walk, Rupert had pointed out a man leaning over the sea wall who was wearing just the kind of sleeveless pullover he would fancy for himself. Alice had said nothing but had smiled and squeezed his arm.

During the years that had passed since Pamela walked in wearing that white coat, Alice had become an expert at her craft. She knew all there was to be known about it. She understood the finer points of grafting, of invisible casting off, of the weaving in of contrasts. She knew every kind of yarn available from top heavyweight natural wool to two-ply cotton and exactly which needles to use with each. Without reference to charts she could tell you that an English size fourteen needle is equivalent to the European two millimetre and the American double O. She could with ease adapt a pattern to a different size or, if necessary, work without a pattern at all. Once she had seen a jumper or cardigan she could copy it and turn out a precisely identical garment. And besides all this, the whole area of knitting was an emotive one to her. She could not help regarding it as having been a life saver and therefore it had become far more to her than some other woman's embroidery or crochet work. So it was natural that on entering a wool shop she should have a sensation of sick excitement as well as experiencing the deep pleasure felt, for example, by a scholar going into a library.

Woolcraft Limited she quickly judged a good shop of its kind and she spent a happy half-hour inside before finally choosing a pattern for a sleeveless pullover and six twenty-five gramme balls of a fine saxe blue wool and acrylic mixture.

There was no opportunity to begin that day. Rupert must have his lunch and then there would be an afternoon's gardening for both of them and in the evening they were going to a dinner-dance in the Pump Room. But on the following afternoon, while Rupert was down the garden trimming the privet hedge, Alice drew out her first ball of blue wool and began.

On moving into the house, she had appropriated the large bottom drawer of a chest in their living room for her knitting materials. In it were all her many leftover balls of wool and ends of wool from a multiplicity of garments made over the years, her gauge, her tape measure, her bodkins for sewing up and her sewing-up skeins and, ranged in front, all her pairs of needles, a pair of every possible size and each pair in its long plastic envelope. Alice had selected a pair of number fourteens, the very finest size for beginning on the welt of Rupert's pullover.

As she cast on the required number of one hundred and fifty stitches and felt the familiar thin metal pins against her hands and the soft, faintly fluffy yarn slip rhythmically between her fingers, a great calm descended upon Alice. It was like coming home after a long absence. It was like having a cigarette (she supposed) or a drink after a month's abstention. It was wonderful. It seemed to set the seal on her happiness. Here she was married, with a charming husband whom she loved, very well off, living in the home of her dreams, and now she was settled in her new life, once more taking up the hobby that afforded her so much pleasure. She had knitted about half an inch, for the work was slow with such fine materials, when she heard Rupert come in from the garden and rinse his hands under the kitchen tap. Presently he walked into the room where she was.

He stood a yard or two in from the doorway and stared at her. 'What are you doing, sweetie?'

'Knitting,' said Alice, smiling at him.

Rupert came and sat opposite her. He was fascinated. He knew there was such a thing as hand-knitting, or that there used to be, for he seemed to remember his mother mentioning it about forty years before, but he had never actually seen it being done. Alice's fingers flicked up and down, making precisely the same movement about a hundred times a minute. And they seemed to move independently of the rest of Alice, of her body which was gracefully relaxed, of her eyes which occasionally met his, and of her mind too, he suspected, which might be wandering off anywhere.

'I didn't know you knitted,' he said after a while.

'Darling! Where do you think your red sweater came from? I told you I made it.'

Rupert had not given much thought to the provenance of the red sweater. 'I suppose I thought you must have done it on a machine,' he said.

Alice laughed heartily at this. She continued to knit. Rupert read the evening paper which had just been delivered. After a time he said, 'Can I talk to you while you're doing that?'

He sounded so like a little boy whose mother cannot be bothered with him that Alice's heart was touched. 'Darling,

of course you can. Talk away! I'm a very practised knitter,
you know. I can not only talk while I'm knitting, I can read,
watch television — my goodness, I could knit in the dark!'
And she fixed her eyes on him, smiling tenderly, while her
fingers jerked up and down like pistons.

But Rupert didn't talk. He hardly said a word until they
were out for their evening walk, and next day when she
again took up the blue pullover she was once more con-
scious of his stare. After a while he lit a cigarette, his first
for several weeks. Without a word he left the room and
when she went into the kitchen to prepare their evening meal
she found him sitting at the table, reading one of his
favourite war memoirs.

It was not until Alice had had four sessions of work on the
pullover and had completed six inches of the back, having
changed by now to a slightly coarser needle, number twelve
and made of red plastic, that Rupert made any further reference to her occupation.

'You know, sweetie,' he said, 'there's absolutely no reason why we shouldn't buy our clothes ready-made. We're
not poor. I hope I haven't given you the impression that I'm
a tight-fisted sort of chap. Any time you want the money to
buy yourself a blouse or a dress or whatever that is, you've
only to say the word.'

'This isn't for me, Rupert, it's for you. You said you
wanted a pullover like the one we saw on that man on the sea
front.'

'Did I? I suppose I must have if you say so but I don't recall it. Anyway, I can pop down to the men's outfitters and
buy one if I feel so inclined, can't I, eh? There's no need for
you to wear yourself out making something I can buy in ten
minutes.'

'But I *like* knitting, darling. I love it. And I think home-
knitted garments are much nicer than bought ones.'

'Must make your fingers ache, I should think,' said Rupert. 'Talk about wearing one's fingers to the bone. I know the meaning of that phrase all right now, eh?'

'Don't be so silly,' snapped Alice. 'Of course it doesn't make my fingers ache. I enjoy it. And I think it's a great pity you've started smoking again.'

Rupert smoked five cigarettes that day and ten the next and the day after that Pamela and Guy came to stay for a fortnight's holiday.

Rupert thought, and Alice agreed with him, that if you lived by the sea it was positively your duty to invite close friends for their summer holidays. Besides, Guy and Pamela, who hadn't a large income, had two children at expensive boarding schools and probably would otherwise have had no holiday at all. They arrived, while their children were away camping, for the middle two weeks of August.

Pamela had not knitted a row since her daughter was two but she liked to watch Alice at work. She said she found it soothing. And when she looked inside the knitting drawer in the chest and saw the leftover hanks of yarn in such delectable shades, pinks and lilacs and subtle greens and honey yellows and chocolate browns, she said it made her feel she must take it up again, for clothes cost so much and it would be a great saving.

Guy was not one of those writers who never speak of their work. He was always entertaining on the subject of the intricate and complex detective stories he yearly produced and would weave plots out of all kinds of common household incidents or create them from things he observed while they were out for a drive. Alice enjoyed hearing him evolve new murder methods and he played up to her with more and more ingenious and bizarre devices.

'Now take warfarin,' he would say. 'They use it to kill rats. It inhibits the clotting of the blood, so that when the rats fight among themselves and receive even a small wound they bleed to death.'

'They give it to human beings too,' said Alice, the nurse.

'Or something very close to it. It stops clots forming in people who've had a thrombosis.'

'Do they now? That's very interesting. If I were going to use that method in a book I'd have the murderer give his victim warfarin plus a strong sedative. Then a small cut, say to the wrist. . .'

Another time he was much intrigued by a book of Alice's on plants inadvisable for use in winemaking. Most illuminating for the thriller writer, he said.

'It says here that the skunk cabbage, whatever that may be, contains irritant crystals of calcium oxalate. If you eat the stuff the inside of your mouth swells up and you die because you can't breathe. Now your average pathologist might notice the swellings but I'd be willing to bet you anything he'd never suppose them the result of eating *lysichiton symplocarpus*. There's another undetectable murder method for you.'

Alice was excited by his ingenuity and Pamela was used to it. Only Rupert, who had perhaps been nearer actual death than any of them, grew squeamish and was not sorry when the two weeks came to an end and Guy and Pamela were gone. Alice too felt a certain relief. It troubled her that her latent sadism, which she recognized for what it was, should be titillated by Guy's inventions. With thankfulness she returned to the gentle placebo of her knitting and took up the blue pullover again, all eight inches of it.

Rupert lit a cigarette.

'I say, I've been thinking, why don't I buy you a knitting machine?'

'I don't want a knitting machine, darling,' said Alice.

'Had a look at one actually while I was out with old Guy one day. A bit pricey but I don't mind that, sweetie, if it makes you happy.'

'I said I don't want a knitting machine. The point is that I like knitting by hand. I've already told you, it's my hobby, it's a great interest of mine. Why do I want a big cumbersome machine that takes up space and makes a noise when I've got my own two hands?'

He was silent. He watched her fingers working.

'As a matter of fact, it's the noise I don't like,' he said.

'What noise?' said Alice, exasperated.

'That everlasting click-click-click.'

'Oh nonsense! You can't possibly hear anything right across the room.'

'I can.'

'You'll get use to it,' said Alice.

But Rupert did not get used to it, and the next time Alice began her knitting he said: 'It's not just the clicking, sweetie, it's the sight of your hands jerking about mechanically all the time. To be perfectly honest with you it gets on my nerves.'

'Don't look then.'

'I can't help it. There's an awful sort of fascination that draws my eyes.'

Alice was beginning to feel nervous herself. A good deal of her pleasure was spoilt by those staring eyes and the knowledge of his dislike of what she did. It began to affect the texture of her work, making her take uneven stitches. She went on rather more slowly and after half an hour she let the nine-inch-long piece of blue fabric and the needles fall into her lap.

'Let's go out to dinner,' said Rupert eagerly. 'We'll go and have a couple of drinks down on the front and then we'll drive over to the Queen's for dinner.'

'If you like,' said Alice.

'And, sweetie, give up that silly old knitting, eh? For my sake? You wouldn't think twice about doing a little thing like that for me, would you?'

A little thing, he called it. Alice thought of it not twice but many times. She hardly thought of anything else and she lay awake for a large part of the night. But next day she did no knitting and she laid away what she had done in the drawer.

Rupert was her husband, and marriage, as she had often heard people say, was a matter of give and take. This she would give to him, remembering all he had given her.

She missed her knitting bitterly. Those years of doing an active job, literally on her feet all day, and those leisure times when her hands had always been occupied, had unfitted her for reading or listening to music or watching television. With idle hands, it was hard for her to keep still. Incessantly, she fidgeted. And when Rupert, who had not once mentioned the sacrifice she had made for him, did at last refer to her knitting, she had an only just controllable urge to hit him.

They were passing, on an evening walk, that men's outfitters of which he had spoken when first he saw knitting in her hands, and there in the window was a heavyweight wool sweater in creamy white with on it an intricate Fair Isle pattern in red and gray.

'Bet you couldn't do that, eh, sweetie? It takes a machine to make a garment like that. I call that a grand job.'

Alice's hands itched to slap his face. She not make that! Why, give her half a chance and she could make it in a week and turn out a far more beautiful piece of work than that object in the window. But her heart yearned after it, for all that. How easily, when she had been allowed to knit, could she have copied it! How marvellously would it have occupied her, working out those checks and chevrons on squared paper, weaving in the various threads with the yarn skilfully hooked round three fingers! She turned away. Was she never to be allowed to knit again? Must she wait until Rupert died before she could take up her needles?

It began to seem to Alice a monstrous cruelty, this thing which her husband had done to her. Why had she been so stupid as to marry someone she had known only three months? She thought she would enjoy punching him with her fists, pummelling his head, until he cried to her to stop and begged her to knit all she liked.

The change Rupert noticed in his wife he did not attribute to the loss of her hobby. He had forgotten about her knitting. He thought she had become irritable and nervous because she was anxious about his smoking — after all, none knew better than she that he shouldn't smoke — and he made a determined effort, his second since his marriage, to give it up.

After five days of total abstention it seemed to him as if every fibre of his body cried out for, yearned for, put out straining anguished stalks for, a cigarette. It was worst of all in the pub on the sea front where the atmosphere was laden with aromatic cigarette smoke, and there, while Alice was sitting at their table, he bought a surreptitious packet of twenty at the bar.

Back home, he took one out and lit it. His need for nicotine was so great that he had forgotten everything else. He had even forgotten that Alice was sitting opposite him. He took a wonderful long inhalation, the kind that makes the room rock and waves roar in one's head, a cool, aromatic, heady, glorious draw.

The next thing he knew the cigarette had been pulled out of his mouth and hurled into the fireplace and Alice was belabouring him with her fists while stamping on the remaining nineteen cigarettes in the packet.

'You mean selfish cruel beast! You can keep on with your filthy evil-smelling addiction that makes me sick to my stomach, you can keep that up, killing yourself, while I'm not allowed to do my poor harmless useful work. You selfish insensitive pig!'

It was their first quarrel and it went on for hours.

Next morning Rupert went into town and bought a hundred cigarettes and Alice locked herself in her bedroom and knitted. They were reconciled after two or three days. Rupert promised to undergo hypnosis for his smoking. Nothing was said at the time about Alice's knitting, but soon afterwards she explained quite calmly and rationally to Rupert that she needed to knit for her 'nerves' and would have to devote specific time to it, such as an hour every evening during which she would go and sit in their little-used dining room.

Rupert said he would miss her. He hadn't got married for his wife to be in one room and he in another. But all right, he hadn't much option, he supposed, so long as it was only an hour.

It began as an hour. Alice found she didn't miss Rupert's company. It seemed to her that they had said to each other all they had to say and all they ever would have. If there had been any excitement in their marriage, there was none left now. Knitting itself was more interesting, though when this garment was completed she would make no more for Rupert. Let him go to his men's outfitters if that was what he wanted. She thought she might make herself a burgundy wool suit. And as she envisaged it, longing to begin, the allotted hour lengthened into an hour and a half, into two.

She had almost completed the back of the pullover after two and a half hours concentrated work, when Rupert burst into the room, a cigarette in his mouth and his breath smelling of whiskey. He snatched the knitting out of her hands and pulled it off the red plastic needles and snapped each needle in half.

Alice screamed at him and seized his collar and began shaking him, but Rupert tore the pattern across and unravelled stitches as fast as he could go. Alice struck him repeatedly across the face. He dodged and hit her such a blow that she fell to the floor, and then he pulled out every one of those two or three hundred rows of knitting until all that remained was a loose and tangled pile of crinkled blue yarn.

Three days later she told him she wanted a divorce. Rupert said she couldn't want one as much as he did. In that case, said Alice, perhaps he would like to pack his things and leave the house as soon as possible.

'Me? Leave this house? You must be joking.'

'Indeed I'm not joking. That's what a decent man would do.'

'What, just walk out of a house I bought with my inheritance from my parents? Walk out on the furniture you bought with my life's savings? You're not only a hysterical bitch, you're out of your mind. *You* can go. I'll pay my maintenance, the law forces me to do that, though it'll be the minimum I can get away with, I promise you.'

'And you call yourself an officer and a gentlemen!' said Alice. 'What am I supposed to do? Go back to nursing? Go back to a poky flat? I'd rather die. Certainly I'm staying in this house.'

They argued about it bitterly day after day. Rupert's need overcame the hypnosis and he chain-smoked. Alice was now afraid to knit in his presence, for he was physically stronger than she, even if she had had the heart to start the blue pullover once again. And whom would she give it to? She would not get out of the house, *her* house which Rupert had given her for which, in exchange, she had given him the most important thing she had.

'I gave up my knitting for you,' she screamed at him, 'and you can't even give me a house and a few sticks of furniture.'

'You're mad,' said Rupert. 'You ought to be locked up.'

Alice rushed at him and smacked his face. He caught her hands and threw her into a chair and slammed out of the room. He went down to the pub on the sea front and had two double whiskies and smoked a packet of cigarettes. When he got back Alice was in bed in the spare room. Just as he refused to leave the house, so Rupert had refused to get out of his own bedroom. He took two sleeping tablets and went to bed.

In the morning Alice went into the room where Rupert was and washed his scalp and combed his beautiful thick white hair. She changed the pillowcases, wiped a spot off Rupert's pyjama jacket and then she phoned the doctor to

say Rupert was dead. He must have passed away in his
sleep. She had awakened to find him dead beside her.

'His heart, of course,' said the doctor, and because Alice
had been a nurse, 'a massive myocardial infarction.'

She nodded. 'I suppose I should have expected it.'

'Well, in these cases. . .'

'You never know, do you? I must be grateful for the few
happy months we had together.'

The doctor signed the death certificate. There was no
question of an autopsy. Pamela and Guy came to the cremation and took Alice back home with them for four weeks.
When Alice left to return to the house that was now entirely
hers they promised to take her at her word and come to stay
once again in the summer. Alice was very comfortably off,
for by no means all Rupert's savings had been spent on the
furniture, his life assurance had been considerable, and
there was his army pension, reduced but still generous.

It was an amazingly young-looking Alice, her hair rinsed
primrose, her figure the trimmest it had been in ten years,
who met Guy and Pamela at the station. She was driving a
new white Lancia coupé and wearing a very smart knitted
suit in a subtle shade of burgundy.

'I love your suit,' said Pamela.

'I made it.'

'I really must take up knitting again. I used to be so good
at it, didn't I? And think of the money one saves.'

On the following evening, a Sunday, after they had spent
most of the day on the beach, Pamela again reverted to the
subject of knitting and said her fingers itched to start on
something straightaway. Alice looked thoughtful. Then she
opened the bottom drawer of the chest and took out the saxe
blue wool.

'You could have this if you like, and this pattern. You
could make it for Guy.'

Pamela took the pattern which had apparently been torn in

half and mended with sticking tape. She looked at the hanks of wool. 'Has some of it been used?'

'I didn't like what I'd done so I undid it. The wool's been washed and carded to get the crinkles out.'

'If you're thinking of making that for me,' said Guy, 'I'm all for it. Splendid idea.'

'All right. Why not? Very fine needles it takes, doesn't it? Have you got a pair of fourteens, Alice?'

A shadow passed across Alice's face. She hesitated. Then she picked up the plastic envelopes one by one, but desultorily, until Pamela, fired now with enthusiasm, dropped on her knees beside her and began hunting through the drawer.

'Here we are. Number fourteen, two millimetres, US double O. . . There's only one needle here, Alice.'

'Sorry about that, it must be lost.' Alice took the single needle from her almost roughly and made as if to close the drawer.

'No, wait a minute, it's bound to be loose in there somewhere.'

'I'm sure it isn't, it's lost. You won't have time to start tonight, anyway.'

Guy said, 'I don't see how you could lose one knitting needle.'

'In a train,' said Pamela, peering into each needle packet. 'It could fall down the side of the seat and before you could get it out you'd be at your station.'

'Alice never goes in trains.'

'I suppose you could use it to unblock a drainpipe?'

'You'd use a big fat one for that. Now if this situation happened in one of my books I'd have it that the needle was a murder weapon. Inserted into the scalp of a person who was, say drugged or drunk, it would penetrate the covering of the brain and the brain itself, causing a subdural haemorrhage. You'd have to sharpen the point a bit, file it maybe, and then of course you'd throw it away afterwards. Hence, you see, only one number fourteen needle in the drawer.'

'And immediately they examined the body they'd find out,' said his wife.

'Well you know, I don't think they would. Did you know that almost all men over middle age have enough signs of coronary disease for a pathologist, unless he was exceptionally thorough, to assume that as the cause of death? Of course your victim would have to have a good head of hair to cover up the mark of entry. . .'

'For heaven's sake, let's change the subject,' said Pamela, closing the drawer, for she had noticed that Alice, perhaps because of that tactless reference to coronaries, had gone very white and that the hands which held the wool were trembling.

But she managed a smile. 'We'll buy you a pair of number fourteens tomorrow,' she said, 'and perhaps I'll start on something new as well. My mother always used to say that the devil finds work for idle hands to do.'

Front Seat

Along the sea front, between the pier and the old town, was a row of wooden seats. There were six of them, regularly spaced on the grass, and they faced the dunes, the sea wall, and the sea. To some people, including Mrs Jones, they were known by name as Fisher, Jackson, Teague, Prendergast, Lubbock and Rupert Moore. It was on this last, the one that was curiously known by the Christian as well as the family name of the man it commemorated, that Mrs Jones invariably chose to sit.

She sat there every day, enjoying the peace and quiet, looking at the sea and thinking about the past. It was most pleasant on mild winter days or on those days of summer when the sky was overcast, for then the holiday visitors stayed in their cars or went off to buy prawns and crabs and expensive knick-knacks. Mrs Jones thought how glad she was that last year, when Mr Jones had been taken from her, she had bought the house in the old town, even though this had meant separating herself from her daughter. She thought about her son in London and her daughter in Ipswich, good loving children that they were, and about her grandchildren, and sometimes about her good fortune in having a comfortable annuity as well as her pension.

But mostly, sitting on Rupert Moore, between Fisher and Teague, she thought about the first man in her life to whom even now, after so long, she always referred to as her darling. She had so accustomed herself to calling him this that to her the endearment had become his name. My darling, thought Mrs Jones, as some other old woman might have thought of John or Charlie or Tom.

She felt closer to him here than anywhere, which was why she chose to rest on this seat and not on one of the others.

On 15 July, St Swithin's Day, Hugh and Cecily Banksome sat in their car, which was parked on the promenade, and looked at the grey choppy sea. Or, rather, Hugh looked at the sea while Cecily looked at Mrs Jones. The temperature was around ten degrees, according to Cecily who moved with the times, or fifty, according to Hugh who did not. It was not yet raining, though the indications were that it soon would be. Hugh was wishing they had gone to the Costa Brava where there would have been high-rise blocks and fish and chips and bull fights, but at least the sun would have shone. Cecily had got it into her head that it was bourgeois and unpatriotic to go abroad for one's holidays.

'I wonder why she always sits there,' said Cecily.

'Who sits where?'

'That old woman. She always sits on that particular seat. She was there yesterday and the day before.'

'Didn't notice,' said Hugh.

'You never notice anything. While you were in the pub yesterday,' said Cecily with emphasis, 'I waited till she'd gone and then I read the inscription on that seat. On the metal plate on the back. D'you know what it says?'

'Of course I don't,' said Hugh, opening the window to let out cigarette smoke. An icy breeze hit him in the face.

'Do close the window. It says: ''Rupert Moore gave this seat to Northwold in thanks for his deliverance. I was in prison and ye came unto me, Matthew, chapter twenty-five, verse thirty-five.'' How about that?'

'Remarkable.' Hugh thought he knew all about being in prison. He looked at his watch. 'Opening time,' he said. 'We can go and get a drink, thank God.'

On the following morning he went out fishing without her. They met in their room before dinner, Hugh bracing himself to face certain sarcastic questions, not without precedent, as to whether he had had a nice day. Forestalling them by telling her they had caught only one small mackerel, for the censure would be greater if he had enjoyed himself, he was soon interrupted.

'I've got the whole story about the seat out of that nice man with the beard.'

Hugh's memory was poor and for a moment he didn't know which seat she was talking about, but he recognized the nice man from her description. A busybody know-all who lived in Northwold and hung about the hotel bar.

'He insisted on buying me a drink. Well, two, as a matter of fact.' She smiled archly and patted her hair as if the bearded know-all had, at the very least, invited her to Aldeburgh for the weekend. 'He's called Arnold Cottle and he said this Rupert Moore put that seat there because he'd murdered his wife. He was put on trial and he was acquitted and that's what it means about "deliverance" and being in prison.'

'You can't say he murdered his wife if he was acquitted.'

'You know what I mean,' said Cecily. 'It was ages ago, in 1930. I mean, I was only a baby.' Hugh thought it wiser not to point out that at ten one is hardly a baby. 'They acquitted him, or he got off on appeal, something like that, and he came back here to live and had that seat put there. Only the local people didn't want a murderer and they broke his windows and called after him in the street and he had to go.'

'Poor devil,' said Hugh.

'Well, I don't know about that, Hugh. From what Arnold said, the case was very unsavoury. Moore was quite young and very good looking and he was a painter, though he had a private income. His poor wife was much older and an invalid. He gave her cyanide they'd got for killing wasps. He gave it to her in a cup of coffee.'

'I thought you said he didn't do it.'

'Everyone *knew* he'd done it. He only got off because the judge misdirected the jury. You can't imagine how anyone would have the nerve to put up a sort of monument, can you, after a thing like that?'

Hugh started to run his bath. Resignedly, he accepted the fact, from past experience, that part of the evening would be spent in the company of Arnold Cottle. Cecily was not, and never had been, particularly flirtatious except in her own imagination. It was not that. Rather it was that she liked to get hold of causes or what she called examples of injustice or outrage and worry at them, roping in to assist her any helper who might be on hand. There had been the banning of the proposed motorway, the petition against the children's playground, the eviction of the squatters down the road. She was not always reactionary, for she worshipped free speech and racial equality and health foods and clean air. She was a woman of principle who threw herself whole-heartedly into upheaval and change and battles that right might be done, and sometimes into cults for the improvement of her soul. The unfortunate part of all this, or one of the unfortunate parts, was that it brought her so often into the company of bores or rogues. Hugh wondered what she was up to now, and why, and hoped it might be, though it seldom was, a flash in the pan.

Two hours later he found himself with his wife and Arnold Cottle, standing on the wet grass and examining the inscription on the Rupert Moore seat. It wasn't yet dark and wouldn't be for an hour. The sky was heavily overcast and the sea the colour of a recently scoured aluminium pot. No one would have supposed, thought Hugh, that somewhere up there in the west was the sun which, contrary to all present evidence, science told him was throwing off light at the rate of two hundred and fifty million tons a minute.

The others were too rapt to be distracted. He had a look at Fisher ('In memory of Colonel Marius Fisher, V.C., D.S.O., 1874–1951') and at Teague ('William James Teague, of this Town, lost at the Battle of Jutland') and then he prodded Rupert Moore and announced, for something to say, 'That's oak.'

'It is indeed, my dear old chap.' Arnold Cottle spoke to Hugh very warmly and kindly, as if he had decided a priori that he was a harmless lunatic. 'You could get oak in those days. This one was made by a chap called Sarafin, Arthur Sarafin. Curious name, eh? Corruption of Seraphim, I daresay. Fine craftsman, lived up the coast at Lowestoft, but he died quite young, more's the pity. My father knew him, had some of the furniture he made. You can see his initials up there where the crossbar at the top joins the post. A.S. in a little circle, see?'

Hugh thought this most interesting. He had done a bit of carpentry himself until Cecily had stopped it on the ground that she needed his workshop for her groups. That had been in the days when she was into Gestalt. Hugh preferred not to think about them. He had a look at Prendergast ('This seat was placed here by the Hon. Clara Prendergast that the weary might find rest') and was about to ask Cottle if this one was oak or teak, when Cecily said: 'Where did he get the cyanide?'

'Moore?' said Cottle. 'It was never actually proved that he did get it. He said they kept some in their garden shed for killing wasps and his wife had taken it herself. In point of fact, Mrs Moore had written to her sister, saying her life wasn't worth living and she wanted to put an end to it. But this gardener chappie said he'd thrown the wasp killing stuff away a year before.'

'It must have come from somewhere,' said Cecily in such a hectoring tone and looking so belligerent that Hugh felt even more sympathy for Rupert Moore.

Cottle didn't seem to mind the tone or the look. 'Moore had been to several chemists' shops in the area, though not actually in Northwold, and tried to buy cyanide, ostensibly for killing wasps. No chemist admitted to having let him have it. There was one in Tarrington, up the coast here, who sold him another kind of vespicide that contained no cyanide and got him to sign the poison book. Dear Cecily, since you're so interested, why don't you read up on the case in the library? Perhaps I might have the pleasure of taking you there tomorrow?'

The offer was accepted with enthusiasm. They all went into the Cross Keys where Hugh bought three rounds of drinks and Arnold Cottle bought none, having failed to bring his wallet with him. Cecily fastened on to the barman and elicited from him that the old woman who always sat on the Rupert Moore seat was called Mrs Jones, that she had come to Northwold the year before from Ipswich and was of Suffolk, though not Northwold, origins.

'Why does she always sit there?'

'Ask me another,' said the barman, presumably meaning this rejoinder rhetorically, which was not the way Cecily took it.

'What's so fascinating about that seat?'

'It seems to fascinate you,' said Hugh. 'Can't you give it a rest? The whole thing's been over and done with for going on fifty years.'

Cecily said, 'There's nothing else to do in this damned place,' which displeased the barman so much that he moved off in a huff. 'I've got a very active brain, Hugh. You ought to know that by now. I'm afraid I'm not content to fuddle it with drink or spend ten hours pulling one poor little fish out of the sea.'

The library visit, from which Hugh was excused, took

place. But books having been secured, a journey had to be made to the house in which Rupert Moore had lived with his wife and painted his pictures and where the crime had been committed. Arnold Cottle seemed delighted at the prospect, especially as the excursion, at Cecily's suggestion, was to include lunch. Hugh had to go because Cecily couldn't drive and he wasn't going to lend his car to Cottle.

The house was a dull and ugly mansion, now used as a children's home. The superintendent (quite reasonably, Hugh thought) refused to let them tour the interior, but he had no objection to their walking round the grounds. It was bitterly cold for the time of year, but not cold enough to keep the children indoors. They tagged around behind Arnold Cottle and the Branksomes, making unfriendly or impertinent remarks. One of them, a boy with red curly hair and a cast in his eye, threw an apple core at Cecily and when reproved, used a word which, though familiar, is still unexpected on the lips of a five-year-old.

They had lunch, and throughout the meal Cecily read aloud extracts from the trial of Rupert Moore. The medical evidence was so unpleasant that Hugh was unable to finish his steak *au poivre*. Cottle drank nearly a whole bottle of Nuits St Georges and had a double brandy with his coffee. Hugh thought about men who had murdered their wives, and how much easier it must have been when you could get wasp killer made out of cyanide and weed killer made of arsenic. But even if he could have got those things, or have pushed Cecily downstairs, or fixed it for the electric wall heater to fall into the bath while she also was in it, he knew he never would. Even if he got away with it, as poor Rupert Moore had done, he would have the shame and the fear and the guilt for the rest of his life, again as had been the case with Rupert Moore.

Not that he had lived for long. 'He died of some kidney disease just twelve months after they let him out,' said Cecily, 'and by then he'd been hounded out of this place. He had Sarafin make that seat and that was about the last thing he ever did in Northwold.' She scanned through the last chapter of her book. 'There doesn't seem to have been any real motive for the murder, Arnold.'

'I suppose he wanted to marry someone else,' said Cottle, swigging brandy. 'I remember my father saying there were rumours he'd had a girlfriend but nobody seemed to know her name and she wasn't mentioned at the trial.'

'She certainly wasn't,' said Cecily, flicking back in her book so rapidly that she nearly knocked Hugh's coffee cup over. 'You mean there was no clue as to who she was? How did the rumours start, then?'

'Dear Cecily, how do rumours ever start? In point of fact, Moore was known often to have been absent from home in the evenings. There was gossip he'd been seen in Clacton with a girl.'

'Fascinating,' said Cecily. 'I shall spend the rest of the day thoroughly studying all this literature. You and Hugh must amuse yourselves on your own.'

After a dreadful afternoon spent listening to Cottle's troubles, how enemies had prevented him making a success of any career, how his two attempts at getting married had been scotched by his mother, and how his neighbours had a vendetta against him, Hugh finally escaped. Though not before he had lent Cottle ten pounds, this being the lowest of the sums his guest had suggested as appropriate. Cecily had a wonderful time, making herself conversant with the Moore case and now she was in the bath. Hugh wondered if a mighty thump on the bedroom side of the bathroom wall would dislodge the heater and make it fall into the water, but this was merely academic speculation.

After dinner he went for a walk on his own in the rain while Cecily made notes — for what purpose Hugh neither knew nor cared. He poked about in the ruins of the castle; he bought two tickets for the repertory theatre on the following night, hoping that the play, though it was called *Murder-on-*

Sea, might distract Cecily; he wandered about the streets of the old town and he had a drink in the Oyster Catcher's Arms. On the whole, he didn't have a bad time.

The morning being better — a pale, sickly sun was shining and making quite attractive tints on the undersides of black clouds — he thought they might go to the beach. But Cecily had other plans. She got him to take her to Tarrington, and in the little shopping centre she left him to his own devices which included buying two pairs of thicker socks. After that, because it was raining again, there was nothing to do but sit in the car park. She kept him waiting two hours.

'What d'you think?' she said. 'I found that chemist, the one that sold Rupert Moore the wasp killer that hadn't got cyanide in it. And, would you believe it, it's still the same firm. The original pharmacist's grandson is the manager.'

'I suppose,' said Hugh, 'that he told you his grandfather had made a deathbed confession he did give Moore the cyanide after all.'

'Do try not to be so silly. I already knew they had cyanide wasp killer in the shop. It said so in the library book. This young man, the grandson, couldn't tell me much, but he did say his grandfather had had a very pretty young girl assistant. How about that?'

'I've noticed that very pretty young girls often do work in chemist's shops.'

'I'm glad you notice something, at any rate. However, she is not the one. The grandson knows her present whereabouts, and she is a Mrs Lewis. So I shall have to look elsewhere.'

'What d'you mean, the one?' said Hugh dismally.

'My next task,' said Cecily, taking no notice, 'will be to hunt for persons in this case of the name of Jones. Young women, that is. I know where to begin now. Sooner or later I shall root out a girl who was an assistant in a chemist's shop at the time and who married a Jones.'

'What for?'

'That right may be done,' said Cecily solemnly. 'That the truth may at last come out. I see it as my mission. You know I always have a mission, Hugh. It was the merest chance we happened to come to Northwold because Diana Richards recommended it. You wanted to go to Lloret de Mar. I feel it was meant we should come here because there was work for me to do. I am convinced Moore was guilty of this crime, but not alone in his guilt. He had a helper who, I believe, is alive at this moment. I'd like you to drive me to Clacton now. I shall begin by interviewing some of the oldest inhabitants.'

So Hugh drove to Clacton where he lost a pound on the fruit machines. Indefatigably, Cecily pursued her investigations.

Mrs Jones came back from morning service at St Mary's and although she was a good walker and not at all tired, for she had slept well ever since she came to Northwold, she sat down for half an hour on her favourite seat. Two other elderly people who had also been in church were sitting on Jackson ('In memory of Bertrand Jackson, 1859–1924, Philanthropist and Lover of the Arts'). Mrs Jones nodded pleasantly at them; but she didn't speak. It wasn't her way to waste in chat time that was more satisfactorily spent in reminiscence.

A pale grey mackerel sky, a fitful sun. Perhaps it would brighten up later. She thought about her daughter who was coming to lunch. Brenda would be tired after the drive, for the children, dears though they were, would no doubt be troublesome in the car. They would all enjoy that nice piece of sirloin and the Yorkshire pudding and the fresh peas and the chocolate ice cream. She had got in a bottle of sherry so that she and Brenda and Brenda's husband could have a glass each before the meal.

Her son and daughter had been very good to her. They knew she had been a devoted wife to their father, and they didn't resent the place in her love she kept for her darling.

Not that she had ever spoken of him in front of their father or of them when they were small. That would have been unkind and in bad taste. But later she had told them about him and told Brenda, in expansive moments, about the long-past happiness and the tragedy of her darling's death, he so young and handsome and gifted. Perhaps, this afternoon when the rest of them were on the beach, she might allow herself the luxury of mentioning him again. Discreetly, of course, because she had always respected Mr Jones and loved him after a fashion, even though he had taken her away to Ipswich and never attained those heights of talent and success her darling would have enjoyed had he lived. Tranquilly, not unhappily, she recalled to her mind his face, his voice, and some of their conversations.

Mrs Jones was disturbed in her reverie by the presence of that tiresome woman. She had seen her before, hanging about on the promenade and once examining the seat Mrs Jones thought of as her own. An ugly, thin, neurotic-looking woman who was sometimes in the company of a sensible elderly man and sometimes with that shameless scrounger, old Cottle's boy, whom Mrs Jones in her old-fashioned way called a barfly. Today, however, she was alone and to Mrs Jones's dismay was approaching her with intent to speak.

'Do excuse me for speaking to you but I've seen you here so often.'

'Oh, yes?' said Mrs Jones. 'I've seen you too. I'm afraid I have to go now. I've guests for lunch.'

'Please don't go. I won't keep you more than a moment. But I must tell you I'm terribly interested in the Moore case. I can't help wondering if you knew him, you're here so much.'

'I knew him,' said Mrs Jones distantly.

'That's terribly exciting.' And the woman did look very excited. 'I suppose you first met him when he came into the shop?'

'That's right,' said Mrs Jones and she got up. 'But I don't

care to talk about it. It's a very long time ago and it's best forgotten. Good morning.'

'Oh, but please. . . !'

Mrs Jones ignored her. She walked far more rapidly than usual, breathing heavily, along the path toward the old town. She was flustered and upset and very put out. To rake up all that now just when she was thinking of the lovely events of that time! For that day, though not, she hoped, for the future, the encounter had spoiled the seat for her.

'Had a good day with Cottle?' said Hugh.

'Don't speak to me about that man. Can you imagine it, I gave him a ring and a woman answered! She turned out to be some creature on holiday like us who was taking him to Lowestoft in her car. I could come too if I liked. No, thank you very much, I said. What about my finding the girl called Jones? I said. And he was pleased to tell me I was getting *obsessional.* So I gave him a piece of my mind, and that's the last of Arnold Cottle.'

And the last of his ten pounds, thought Hugh. 'So you went on the beach instead?'

'I did not. While you were out in that boat I researched on my own. And most successfully, I may add. You remember that old man in Clacton, the one in the old folks' home? Well, he was quite fit enough to see me today, and I questioned him exhaustively.'

Hugh said nothing. He could guess which of them had been exhausted.

'Ultimately,' said Cecily, 'I was able to prod him into remembering. I asked him to try and recall everyone he had ever known called Jones. And at last he remembered a local policeman, Constable Jones, who got married in or around 1930. And the girl he married worked in *a local chemist's shop.* How about that?'

'You mean she was Moore's girlfriend?'

'Isn't it obvious? Her name was Gladys Palmer. She is now Mrs Jones. Moore was seen about with a girl in Clacton. This girl lived in Clacton and worked in a Clacton chemist's shop. Now it's quite evident that Moore was having a love affair with Gladys Palmer and that he persuaded her to give him the cyanide from the shop where she worked. The *real* evidence is that, according to all the books, that was one of the few chemist's shops from which Moore *never tried to obtain cyanide!*'

'That's real evidence?' said Hugh.

'Of course it is, to anyone with any deductive powers. Gladys Palmer took fright when Moore was found guilty, so she married a policeman for protection, and the policeman's name was Jones. Isn't that proof?'

'Proof of what?'

'Don't you ever remember anything? The barman in that Cross Keys place told us the old woman who sits on the Rupert Moore seat was a Mrs Jones.' Cecily smiled triumphantly. 'They are one and the same.'

'But it's a very common name.'

'Maybe. But Mrs Jones had admitted it. I spoke to her this morning before I went to Clacton. She has admitted knowing Moore and that she first met him when he came into the shop. How about that? And she was very nervous and upset, I can tell you, as well she might be.'

Hugh stared at his wife. He didn't at all like the turn things were taking. 'Cecily, it may be so. It looks like it, but it's not business of ours. I wish you'd leave it.'

'Leave it! For nearly fifty years this woman had got off scot-free when she was as much guilty of the murder of Mrs Moore as Moore was, and you say leave it! It's her guilt brings her to that seat day after day, isn't it? Any psychologist would tell you that.'

'She must be at least seventy. Surely she can be left in peace now?'

'I'm afraid it's much too late for that, Hugh. There must be an inquiry, all the facts must come out. I have written three letters, one to the Home Secretary, one to the Chief

Commissioner at Scotland Yard, and a third to the author of
this very incomplete book. There they are on the dressing
table. Perhaps you's like to look at them while I have my
bath.'

Hugh looked at them. If he were to tear them up she
would only write them again. If he walked into the bathroom
now and dislodged the heater from the wall and it fell into
the water, and she died and it was called an accident. . .
The letters would never be sent, he could have his workshop
back, he could chat up pretty girls who worked in chemist's
shops and go on holiday to the Costa Brava and be free. He
sighed heavily and went down to the bar to get a drink.

Thank goodness, thought Mrs Jones, that woman wasn't
anywhere to be seen this morning. The intrusion of yesterday had upset her for hours, even after Brenda arrived, but
she was getting over it now. Unfortunately in a way, the
weather had taken a turn for the better, and several of the
seats were occupied. But not Rupert Moore. Mrs Jones sat
down on it and put her shopping bag on the ground at her
feet.

She was aware of the proximity of the barfly who was sitting on Lubbock ('Elizabeth Anne Lubbock, for many years
Headmistress of Northwood Girls' High School') and with
him was a different woman, much younger than the other
and very well dressed. With an effort, Mrs Jones expelled
them from her mind. She looked at the calm blue sea and felt
the warm and firm pressure of the oak against her back and
thought about her darling. How sweet their love and com-
panionship had been! It had endured for such a short time,
and then separation and the unbearable loneliness. But she
had been right to marry Mr Jones, for he had been a good
husband and she the wife he wanted, and without him there
would have been no Brian and no Brenda and no money to
buy the house and come here every day to remember. If her
darling had lived, though, and the children had been his, and

if she had had him to sit beside her on his seat and be the joy of her old age. . .

'Do forgive me,' said a voice, 'but I'm a local man myself and I happened to be in Lowestoft yesterday and someone told me they'd heard you'd come back to this part of the world to live.'

Mrs Jones looked at the barfly. Was there to be no end to this kind of thing?

'I've seen you on this seat and I did wonder, and when this friend in Lowestoft told me your present name, all was made plain.'

'I see,' said Mrs Jones, gathering up her shopping bag.

'I want you to know how greatly I admire his work. My father had some charming examples of it — all sold now, alas — and anyone can see that this seat was made by a craftsman compared with the others.' Her stony face, her hostility, made him hesitate. 'You are,' he said, 'who I think you are, aren't you?'

'Of course I am,' said Mrs Jones crossly, another morning spoilt. 'Arthur Sarafin was my first husband. And now I really must be on my way.'

Paintbox Place

Elderly ladies as detectives are not unknown in fiction. Avice Julian could think of two or three, the creations of celebrated authors, and no doubt there were more. It would seem that the quiet routine of an old woman's life, her penchant for gossip and knitting and her curiosity, born of boredom, provide a suitable climate for the consideration of motive and the assessment of clues. In fiction, that is. Would it, Mrs Julian sometimes wondered, also be true in reality?

She took a personal interest. She was eighty-four years old, thin, sharp-witted, arthritic, cantankerous and intolerant. Most of her time she spent sitting in an upright chair in the bay window of her drawing room in her very large house, observing what her neighbours got up to. From the elderly ladies of mystery fiction, though, she differed in one important respect. They were spinsters, she was a widow. In fact, she had been twice married and twice widowed. Could that, she asked herself after reading a particular apposite detective novel, be of significance? Could it affect the deductive powers and it be her spinsterhood which made Miss

Marple, say, a detective of genius? Perhaps. Anthropologists say (Mrs Julian was an erudite person) that in ancient societies maidenhood was revered as having awesome and unique powers. It might be that this was true and that prolonged virginity, though in many respects disagreeable, only serves to enhance them. Possibly, one day, she would have an opportunity to put to the test the Aged Female Sleuth Theory. She saw enough from her window, sitting there knitting herself a twinset in dark blue two-ply. Mostly she eyed the block of houses opposite, on the other side of broad, tree-lined Abelard Avenue.

There were six of them, all joined together, all exactly the same. They all had three storeys, plate-glass windows, a bit of concrete to put the car on, a flowerbed, an outside cupboard to put parcels in and an outside cupboard to put the rubbish sack in. Mrs Julian thought that unhygienic. She had an old-fashioned dustbin, though she had to keep a black plastic bag inside it if she wanted Northway Borough Council to collect her rubbish.

The houses had been built on the site of an old mansion. There had been several such in Abelard Avenue, as well as big houses like Mrs Julian's which were not quite mansions. Most of these had been pulled down and those which remained converted into flats. They would do that to hers when she was gone, thought Mrs Julian, those nephews and nieces and great nephews and great nieces of hers would do that. She had watched the houses opposite being built. About ten years ago it had been. She called them the paintbox houses because there was something about them that reminded her of a child's drawing and because each had its front door painted a different colour, yellow, red, blue, lime, orange and chocolate.

'It's called Paragon Place,' said Mrs Upton, her cleaner and general help, when the building was completed.

'What a ridiculous name! Paintbox Place would be far more suitable.'

Mrs Upton ignored this as she ignored all of Avice Julian's remarks which she regarded as 'showing off', affected or just plain senile. 'They do say,' she said, 'that the next thing'll be they'll start building on that bit of waste ground next door.'

'Waste ground?' said Mrs Julian distantly. 'Can you possibly mean the wood?'

'Waste ground' had certainly been a misnomer, though 'wood' was an exaggeration. It was a couple of rustic acres, more or less covered with trees of which part of one side bordered Mrs Julian's garden, part the Great North Road, and which had its narrow frontage on Abelard Avenue. People used the path through it as a short cut from the station. At Mrs Upton's unwelcome forebodings, Avice Julian had got up and gone to the right hand side of the bay window which overlooked the 'wood' and thought how disagreeable it would be to have another Paintbox Place on her back doorstep. In these days when society seemed to have gone mad, when the cost of living was frightening, when there were endless strikes and she was asked to pay 98 per cent income tax on the interest on some of her investments, it was quite possible, anything could happen.

However, no houses were built next door to Mrs Julian. It appeared that the 'wood', though hardly National Trust or an Area of Outstanding Natural Beauty, was nevertheless scheduled as 'not for residential development'. For her lifetime, it seemed, she would look out on birch trees and green turf and small hawthorn bushes — when she was not, that is, looking out on the inhabitants of Paintbox Place, on Mr and Mrs Arnold and Mr Laindon and the Nicholsons, all young people, none of them much over forty. Their activities were of absorbing interest to Mrs Julian as she knitted away in dark blue two-ply, and a source too of disapproval and sometimes outright condemnation.

After Christmas, in the depths of the winter, when Mrs. Julian was in the kitchen watching Mrs Upton peeling potatoes for lunch, Mrs Upton said: 'You're lucky I'm private, have you thought of that?'

This was beyond Mrs Julian's understanding. 'I beg your pardon?'

'I mean it's lucky for you I'm not one of those council home helps. They're all coming out on strike, the lot of them coming out. They're NUPE, see? Don't you read your paper?'

Mrs Julian certainly did read her paper, the *Daily Telegraph,* which was delivered to her door each morning. She read it from cover to cover after she had had her breakfast, and she was well aware that the National Union of Public Employees was making rumbling noises and threatening to bring its members out over a pay increase. It was typical, in her view, of the age in which she found herself living. Someone or other was always on strike. But she had very little idea of how to identify the Public Employee and had hoped the threatened action would not affect her. To Mrs Upton she said as much.

'Not affect you?' said Mrs Upton, furiously scalping brussels sprouts. She seemed to find Mrs Julian's innocence uproariously funny. 'Well, there'll be no gritters on the roads for a start and maybe you've noticed it's snowing again. Gritters are NUPE. They'll have to close the schools so there'll be kids all over the streets. School caretakers are NUPE. No ambulances if you fall on the ice and break your leg, no hospital porters, and what's more, no dustmen. We won't none of us get our rubbish collected on account of dustmen are NUPE. So how about that for not affecting you?'

Mrs Julian's dustbin, kept just inside the front gate on a concrete slab and concealed from view by a laurel bush and a cotoneaster, was not emptied that week. On the following Monday she looked out of the right hand side of the bay window and saw under the birch trees, on the frosty ground, a dozen or so black plastic sacks, apparently filled with rubbish, their tops secured with wire fasteners. There was no end to the propensities of some people for making disgusting litter, thought Mrs Julian, give them half a chance. She would telephone Northway Council, she would telephone the police. But first she would put on her squirrel coat and take her stick and go out and have a good look.

The snow had melted, the pavement was wet. A car had pulled up and a young woman in jeans and a pair of those silly boots that came up to the thighs like in a pantomime was taking two more black plastic sacks out of the back of it. Mrs Julian was on the point of telling her in no uncertain terms to remove her rubbish at once, when she caught sight of a notice stuck up under the trees. The notice was of ply-wood with printing on it in red chalk: *Northway Council Refuse Tip. Bags This Way.*

Mrs Julian went back into her house. She told Mrs Upton about the refuse tip and Mrs Upton said she already knew but hadn't told Mrs. Julian because it would only upset her.

'You don't know what the world's coming to, do you?' said Mrs Upton, opening a tin of peaches for lunch.

'I most certainly do know,' said Mrs Julian. 'Anarchy. Anarchy is what it is coming to.'

Throughout the week the refuse on the tip mounted. Fortunately, the weather was very cold; as yet there was no smell. In Paintbox Place black plastic sacks of rubbish began to appear outside the cupboard doors, on the steps beside the coloured front doors, overflowing into the narrow flowerbeds. Mrs Upton came five days a week but not on Saturdays or Sundays. When the doorbell rang at ten on Saturday morning Mrs Julian answered it herself and there outside was Mr Arnold from the house with the red front door, behind him on the gravel drive a wheelbarrow containing five black plastic sacks of rubbish.

He was a good-looking, cheerful, polite man was Mr Arnold. Forty-two or three, she supposed. Sometimes she fancied she had seen a melancholy look in his eyes. No wonder, she could well understand if he was melancholic. He said good morning, and he was on his way to the tip with his rubbish and Mr Laindon's and could he take hers too?

'That's very kind and thoughtful of you, Mr. Arnold,' said Mrs Julian. 'You'll find my bag inside the dustbin at the gate. I do appreciate it.'

'No trouble,' said Mr Arnold. 'I'll make a point of collecting your bag, shall I, while the strike lasts?'

Mrs Julian thought. A plan was forming in her mind. 'That won't be necessary, Mr Arnold. I shall be disposing of my waste by other means. Composting, burning,' she said, 'beating tins flat, that kind of thing. Now if everyone were to do the same. . .'

'Ah, life's too short for that, Mrs Julian,' said Mr Arnold and he smiled and went off with his wheelbarrow before she could say what was on the tip of her tongue, that it was shorter for her than for most people.

She watched him take her sack out of the dustbin and trundle his barrow up the slope and along the path between the wet black mounds. Poor man. Many an evening, when Mr Arnold was working late, she had seen the chocolate front door open and young Mr Laindon, divorced, they said, just before he came there, emerge and tap at the red front door and be admitted. Once she had seen Mrs Arnold and Mr Laindon coming back from the station together, taking the short cut through the 'wood'. They had been enjoying each other's company and laughing, though it had been cold and quite late, all of ten at night. And here was Mr Arnold performing kindly little services for Mr Laindon, all innocent of how he was deceived. Or perhaps he was not quite innocent, not ignorant and that accounted for his sad eyes. Perhaps he was like Othello who doted yet doubted, suspected yet strongly loved. It was all very disagreeable, thought Avice Julian, employing one of her favourite words.

She went back into the kitchen and examined the boiler, a

small coke-burning furnace disused since 1963 when the late Alexander Julian had installed central heating. The chimney, she was sure, was swept, the boiler could be used again. Tins could be hammered flat and stacked temporarily in the garden shed. And — why not? — she would start a compost heap. No one should be without a compost heap at the best of times, any alternative was most wasteful.

Her neighbours might contribute to the squalor; she would not. Presently she wrapped herself up in her late husband's Burberry and made her way down to the end of the garden. On the 'wood' side, in the far corner, that would be the place. Up against the fence, thought Mrs Julian. She found a bundle of stout sticks in the shed — Alexander had once grown runner beans up them — and selecting four of these, managed to drive them into the soft earth, one at each of the angles of a roughly conceived square. Next, a strip of chicken wire went round the posts to form an enclosure. She would get Mrs Upton to buy her some garotta next time she went shopping. Avice Julian knew all about making compost heaps, she and her first husband had been experts during the war.

In the afternoon, refreshed by a nap, she emptied the vegetable cupboard and found some strange potatoes growing stems and leaves and some carrots covered in blue fur. Mrs Upton was not a hygienic housekeeper. The potatoes and carrots formed the foundation of the new compost heap. Mrs Julian pulled up a handful of weeds and scattered them on the top.

'I shall have my work cut out, I can see that,' said Mrs Upton on Monday morning. She laughed unpleasantly. 'I'm sure I don't know when the cleaning'll get done if I'm traipsing up and down the garden path all day long.'

Between them they got the boiler alight and fed it Saturday's *Daily Telegraph* and Sunday's *Observer*. Mrs Upton hammered out a can that had contained baked beans and banged her thumb. She made a tremendous fuss about it which Mrs Julian tried to ignore. Mrs Julian went back to her window, cast on for the second sleeve of the dark blue two-ply jumper, and watched women coming in cars with their rubbish sacks for the tip. Some of them hardly bothered to set foot on the pavement but opened the boots of their cars and hurled the sacks from where they stood. With extreme distaste, Mrs Julian watched one of these sacks strike the trunk of a tree and burst open, scattering tins and glass and peelings and leavings and dregs and grounds in all directions.

During the last week of January, Mrs Julian always made her marmalade. She saw no reason to discontinue this custom because she was eighty-four. Grumbling and moaning about her back and varicose veins, Mrs Upton went out to buy preserving sugar and Seville oranges. Mrs Julian peeled potatoes and prepared a cabbage for lunch, carrying the peelings and the outer leaves down the garden to the compost heap herself. Most of the orange peel would go on there in due course. Mrs Julian's marmalade was the clear jelly kind with only strands of rind in it, pared hair-thin.

They made the first batch in the afternoon. Mr Arnold called on the following morning with his barrow. 'Your private refuse operative, Mrs Julian, at your service.'

'Ah, but I've done what I told you I should do,' she said and insisted on his coming down the garden with her to see the compost heap.

'You eat a lot of oranges,' said Mr Arnold.

Then she told him about the marmalade and Mr Arnold said he had never tasted home-made marmalade, he didn't know people made it any more. This shocked Mrs Julian and rather confirmed her opinion of Mrs Arnold. She gave him a jar of marmalade and he was profuse in his thanks.

She was glad to get indoors again. The meteorological people had been right when they said there was another cold spell coming. Mrs Julian knitted and looked out of the window and saw Mrs Arnold brought back from somewhere or other by Mr Laindon in his car. By lunchtime it had begun to snow. The heavy, grey, louring sky looked full of snow.

This did not deter Mrs Julian's great-niece from dropping in unexpectedly with her boyfriend. They said frankly that they had come to look at the rubbish tip which was said to be the biggest in London apart from the one which filled the whole of Leicester Square. They stood in the window staring at it and giggling each time anyone arrived with fresh offerings.

'It's surrealistic!' shrieked the great-niece as a sack, weighted down with snow, rolled slowly out of the branches of a tree where it had been suspended for some days. 'It's fantastic! I could stand here all day just watching it.'

Mrs Julian was very glad that she did not but departed after about an hour (with a jar of marmalade) to something called the Screen on the Hill which turned out to be a cinema in Hampstead. After they had gone it snowed harder than ever. There was a heavy frost that night and the next.

'You don't want to set foot outside,' said Mrs Upton on Monday morning. 'The pavements are like glass.' And she went off into a long tale about her son Stewart who was a police constable finding an old lady who had slipped over and was lying helpless on the ice.

Mrs Julian nodded impatiently. 'I have no intention whatsoever of going outside. And you must be very careful when you go down that path to the compost heap.'

They made a second batch of marmalade. The boiler refused to light so Mrs Julian said to leave it but try it again tomorrow, for there was quite an accumulation of newspapers to be burnt. Mrs Julian sat in the window, sewing together the sections of the dark blue two-ply jumper and watching the people coming through the snow to the refuse tip. Capped with snow, the mounds on the tip resembled a mountain range. In the Arctic perhaps, thought Mrs Julian fancifully, or on some planet where the temperature was always sub-zero.

All the week it snowed and froze and snowed and melted and froze again. Mrs Julian stayed indoors. Her nephew, the one who wrote science fiction, phoned to ask if she was all right, and her other nephew, the one who was a commercial photographer, came round to sweep her drive clear of snow. By the time he arrived Mr Laindon had already done it, but Mrs Julian gave him a jar of marmalade just the same. She had resisted giving one to Mr Laindon because of the way he carried on with Mrs Arnold.

It started thawing on Saturday. Mrs Julian sat in the window, casting on for the left front of her cardigan and watching the snow and ice drip away and flow down the gutters. She left the curtains undrawn, as she often did, when it got dark.

At about eight Mrs Arnold came out of the red front door and Mr Laindon came out of the chocolate front door and they stood chatting and laughing together until Mr Arnold came out. Mr Arnold unlocked the doors of his car and said something to Mr Laindon. How Mrs Julian wished she could have heard what it was! Mr Laindon only shook his head. She saw Mrs Arnold get quickly into the car and shut the door. Very cowardly, not wanting to get involved, thought Mrs Julian. Mr Arnold was arguing now with Mr Laindon, trying to persuade him to something, apparently. Perhaps to leave Mrs Arnold alone. But all Mr Laindon did was give a silly sort of laugh and retreat into the house with the chocolate door. The Arnolds went off, Mr Arnold driving quite recklessly fast in this sort of weather, as if he were fearfully late for wherever they were going or, more likely, in a great rage.

Mrs Julian saw nothing of Mr Laindon on the following day, the Sunday, but in the afternoon she saw Mrs Arnold go out on her own. She crossed the road from Paintbox Place and took the path, still mercifully clear of rubbish sacks, through the 'wood' towards the station. Off to a secret assignation, Mrs Julian supposed. The weather was

drier and less cold but she felt no inclination to go out. She
sat in the window, doing the ribbing part of the left front of
her cardigan and noting that the rubbish sacks were mount-
ing again in Paintbox Place. For some reason, laziness perhaps, Mr Arnold had failed to clear them away on Saturday
morning. Mrs Julian had a nap and a cup of tea and read the
Observer.

It pleased her that Mrs Upton had burnt up all the old
newspapers. At any rate, there were none to be seen. But
what had she done with the empty tins? Mrs Julian looked
everywhere for the hammered-out, empty tins. She looked
in the kitchen cupboards and the cupboards under the stairs
and even in the dining room and the morning room. You
never knew with people like Mrs Upton. Perhaps she had
put them in the shed, perhaps she had actually done what her
employer suggested and put them in the shed.

Mrs Julian went back to the living room, back to her window, and got there just in time to see Mr Arnold letting himself into his house. Time tended to pass slowly for her at
weekends and she was surprised to find it was as late as nine
o'clock. It had begun to rain. She could see the slanting rain
shining gold in the light from the lamps in Paintbox Place.

She sat in the window and picked up her knitting. After a
little while the red front door opened and Mr Arnold came
out. He had changed out of his wet clothes, changed grey
trousers for dark brown, blue jacket for sweater and anorak.
He took hold of the nearest rubbish sack and dragged it just
inside the door. Within a minute or two he had come out
again, carrying the sack, which he loaded onto the barrow
he fetched from the parking area.

It was at this point that Mrs Julian's telephone rang. The
phone was at the other end of the room. Her caller was the
elder of her nephews, the commercial photographer, wanting to know if he might borrow pieces from her Second Em-
pire bedroom furniture for some set or background. They
had all enjoyed the marmalade, it was nearly gone. Mrs Ju-

lian said he should have another jar of marmalade next year but he certainly could not borrow her furniture. She didn't want pictures of her wardrobe and dressing table all over those vulgar magazines, thank you very much. When she returned to her point of vantage at the window Mr Arnold had disappeared.

Disappeared, that is, from the forecourt of Paintbox Place. Mrs Julian crossed to the right hand side of the bay to draw the curtains and shut out the rain, and there he was scaling the wet slippery black mountains, clutching a rubbish sack in his hand. The sack looked none too secure, for its side had been punctured by the neck of a bottle and its top was fastened not with a wire fastener but wound round and round with blue string. Finally, he dropped it at the side of one of the high mounds round the birch tree. Mrs Julian drew the curtains.

Mrs Upton arrived punctually in the morning, agog with her news. It was a blessing she had such a strong constitution, Mrs Julian thought. Many a woman of her advanced years would have been made ill — or worse — by hearing a thing like that.

'How can you possibly know?' she said. 'There's nothing in this morning's paper.'

Stewart, of course. Stewart, the policeman.

'She was coming home from the station,' said Mrs Upton, 'through that bit of waste ground.' She cocked a thumb in the direction of the 'wood'. 'Asking for trouble, wasn't she? Nasty dark lonely place. This chap, whoever he was, he clouted her over the head with what they call a blunt instrument. That was about half-past eight, though they never found her till ten. Stewart says there was blood all over, turned him up proper it did, and him used to it.'

'What a shocking thing,' said Mrs Julian. 'What a dreadful thing. Poor Mrs Arnold.'

'Murdered for the cash in her handbag, though there wasn't all that much. No one's safe these days.'

When such an event takes place it is almost impossible for some hours to deflect one's thoughts onto any other subject. Her knitting lying in her lap, Mrs Julian sat in the window, contemplating the paintbox houses. A vehicle that was certainly a police car, though it had no blue lamp, arrived in the course of the morning and two policemen in plain clothes were admitted to the house with the red front door. Presumably by Mr Arnold who was not, however, visible to Mrs Julian.

What must it be like to lose, in so violent a manner, one's marriage partner? Even so unsatisfactory a marriage partner as poor Mrs Arnold had been. Did Mr Laindon know? Mrs Julian wondered. She found herself incapable of imagining what his feelings must be. No one came out of or went into any of the houses in Paintbox Place and at one o'clock Mrs Julian had to leave her window and go into the dining room for lunch.

'Of course you know what the police always say, don't you?' said Mrs Upton, sticking a rather underdone lamb chop down in front of her. 'The husband's always the first to be suspected. Shows marriage up in a shocking light, don't you reckon?'

Mrs Julian made no reply but merely lifted her shoulders. Both her husbands had been devoted to and she told herself that she had no personal experience of the kind of uncivilized relationship Mrs Upton was talking about. But could she say the same for Mrs Arnold? Had she not, in fact, for weeks, for months, now been deploring the state of the Arnolds' marriage and even awaiting some fearful climax?

It was at this point, or soon after when she was back in her window, that Avice Julian began to see herself as a possible Miss Marple or Miss Silver, though she had not recently been reading the works of either of those ladies' creators. Rather it was that she saw the sound commonsense which lay behind the notion of elderly women as detectives. Who else has the leisure to be so observant? Who else had behind them a lifetime of knowledge of human nature? Who else has suffered sufficient disillusionment to be able to face so squarely such unpalatable facts?

Beyond a doubt, the facts Mrs Julian was facing were unpalatable. Nevertheless, she marshalled them. Mrs Arnold had been an unfaithful wife. She had been conducting some sort of love affair with Mr Laindon. That Mr Arnold had not known of it was evident from her conduct of this extra-marital adventure in his absence. That he was beginning to be aware of it was apparent from his behaviour of Saturday evening. What more probable than that he had set off to meet his wife at the station on Sunday evening, had quarrelled with her about this very matter, and had struck her down in a jealous rage? When Mrs Julian had seen him first he had been running home from the scene of the crime, clutching to him under his jacket the weapon for which Mrs Upton said the police were now searching.

The morning had been dull and damp but after lunch it had dried up and a weak, watery sun came out. Mrs Julian put on her squirrel coat and went out into the garden, the first time she had been out for nine days.

The compost heap had not increased much in size. Perhaps the weight of snow had flattened it down or, more likely, Mrs Upton had failed in her duty. Displeased, Mrs Julian went back into the front garden and down to the gate where she lifted the lid of her dustbin, confident of what she would find inside. But, no, she had done Mrs Upton an injustice. The dustbin was empty and quite clean. She stood by the fence and viewed the tip.

What an eyesore it was! A considerable amount of leakage, due to careless packing and fastening, had taken place and the wet, fetid, black hillocks were strewn all over with torn and soggy paper, cartons and packages, while in the valleys between clustered like some evil growth, a conglomeration of decaying fruit and vegetable parings, mildewed bread, tea leaves, coffee grounds and broken glass. In one

hollow there was movement. Maggots or the twitching nose
of a rat? Mrs Julian shuddered and looked hastily away. She
raised her eyes to take in the continued presence under the
birch tree of the sack Mr Arnold had deposited there on the
previous evening, the sack that was punctured by the neck of
a bottle and bound with blue string.

She returned to the house. Was she justified in keeping
this knowledge of hers to herself? There was by then no
doubt in her mind as to what Mr Arnold had done. After killing his wife he had run home, changed his bloodstained
clothes for clean ones and, fetching in the rubbish sack from
outside, inserted into it the garments he had just removed
and the blunt instrument, so-called, he had used. An iron bar
perhaps or a length of metal piping he had picked up in the
'wood'. In so doing he had mislaid the wire fastener and
could find no other, so he had been obliged to fasten the sack
with the nearest thing to hand, a piece of string. Then across
the road with it as he had been on several previous occasions, this time to deposit there a sack containing evidence
that would incriminate him if found on his property. But
what could be more anonymous than a black plastic sack on
a council refuse tip? There it would be only one among a
thousand and, he must have supposed, impossible to identify.

Mrs Julian disliked the idea of harming her kind and
thoughtful neighbour. But justice must be done. If she was
in possession of knowledge the police could not otherwise
acquire, it was plainly her duty to reveal it. And the more
she thought of it the more convinced she was that there was
the correct solution to the crime against Mrs Arnold. Would
not Miss Seaton have thought so? Would not Miss Marple,
having found parallels between Mr Arnold's behaviour and
that of some St Mary Mead husband, having considered and
weighed the awful significance of the quarrel on Saturday
night and the extraordinary circumstance of taking rubbish

to a tip at nine-thirty on a wet Sunday evening, would she not have laid the whole matter before the CID?

She hesitated for only a few minutes before fetching the telephone directory and looking up the number. By three o'clock in the afternoon she was making a call to her local police station.

The detective sergeant and constable who came to see Mrs Julian half an hour later showed no surprise at being supplied with information by such as she. Perhaps they too read the works of the inventors of elderly lady sleuths. They treated Mrs Julian with great courtesy and after she had told them what she suspected they suggested she accompany them to the vicinity of the tip and point out the incriminating sack.

However, it was quite possible for her to do this from the right-hand side of the bay window. The detectives nodded and wrote things in notebooks and thanked her and went away, and after a little while a van arrived and a policeman in uniform got out and removed the sack. Mrs Julian sat in the window, working away at the lacy pattern on the front of her dark blue cardigan and watching for the arrest of Mr Arnold. She watched with trepidation and fear for him and a reluctant sympathy. There were policemen about the area all day, tramping around among the rubbish sacks, investigating gardens and ringing doorbells, but none of them went to arrest Mr Arnold.

Nothing happened at all apart from Mr Laindon calling at eight in the evening. He seemed very upset and his face looked white and drawn. He had come, he said, to ask Mrs Julian if she would care to contribute to the cost of a wreath for Mrs Arnold or would she be sending flowers personally?

'I should prefer to see to my own little floral tribute,' said Mrs Julian rather frostily.

'Just as you like, of course. I'm really going round asking people to give myself something to do. I feel absolutely bowled over by this business. They were wonderful to me, the Arnolds, you know. You couldn't have better friends. I was feeling pretty grim when I first came here — my divorce and all that — and the Arnolds, well, they looked after me like a brother, never let me be on my own, even insisted I go out with them. And now a terrible thing like this has to happen and to a wonderful person like that. . .'

Mrs Julian had no wish to listen to this sort of thing. No doubt, there were some gullible enough to believe it. She went to bed wondering if the arrest would take place during the night, discreetly, so that the neighbours should not witness it.

The paintbox houses looked just the same in the morning. But of course they would. The arrest of Mr Arnold would hardly affect their appearance. The phone rang at 9:30 and Mrs Upton took the call. She came into the morning room where Mrs Julian was finishing her breakfast.

'The police want to come round and see you again. I said I'd ask. I said you mightn't be up to it, not being so young as you used to be.'

'Neither are you or they,' said Mrs Julian and then she spoke to the police herself and told them to come whenever it suited them.

During the next half hour some not disagreeable fantasies went round in Mrs Julian's head. Such is often the outcome of identifying with characters in fiction. She imagined herself congratulated on her acumen and even, on a future occasion when some other baffling crime had taken place, consulted by policemen of high rank. Mrs Upton had served her well on the whole, as well as could be expected in these trying times. Perhaps one day, when it came to the question of Stewart's promotion, a word from her in the right place. . .

The doorbell rang. It was the same detective sergeant and detective constable. Mrs Julian was a little disappointed, she thought she rated an inspector now. They greeted her with jovial smiles and invited her into her own kitchen where they said they had something to show her. Between them they were lugging a large canvas bag.

The sergeant asked Mrs Upton if she could find them a sheet of newspaper, and before Mrs Julian could say that they had burnt all the newspapers, Saturday's *Daily Telegraph* was produced from where it had been secreted. Then, to Mrs Julian's amazement, he pulled out of the canvas bag the black plastic rubbish sack, punctured on one side and secured at the top with blue string, which she had seen Mr Arnold deposit on the tip on Sunday evening.

'I hope you won't find it too distasteful, madam,' he said, 'just to cast your eyes over some of the contents of this bag.'

Mrs Julian was astounded that he should ask such a thing of someone of her age. But she indicated with a faint nod and wave of her hand that she would comply, while inwardly she braced herself for the sight of some hideous bludgeon, perhaps encrusted with blood and hair, and for the emergence from the depths of the sack of a bloodstained jacket and pair of trousers. She would not faint or cry out, she was determined on that, whatever she might see.

It was the constable who untied the string and spread open the neck of the sack. With care, the sergeant began to remove its contents and to drop them on the newspaper Mrs Upton had laid on the floor. He dropped them, in so far as he could, in small separate heaps: a quantity of orange peel, a few lengths of dark blue two-ply knitting wool, innumerable Earl Grey tea bags, potato peelings, cabbage leaves, a lamb chop bone, the sherry bottle whose neck had pierced the side of the sack, and seven copies of the *Daily Telegraph* with one of the *Observer,* all with 'Julian, 1 Abelard Avenue' scrawled above the masthead. . .

Mrs Julian surveyed her kitchen floor. She looked at the sergeant and the constable and at the yard or so of dark blue two-ply knitting wool which he still held in his hand and which he had unwound from the neck of the sack.

'I fail to understand,' she said.

'I'm afraid this sack would appear to contain waste from your own household, Mrs Julian,' said the sergeant. 'In other words to have been yours and been disposed of from your premises.'

Mrs Julian sat down. She sat down rather heavily on one of the bentwood chairs and fixed her eyes on the opposite wall and felt a strange tingling hot sensation in her face that she hadn't experienced for some sixty years. She was blushing.

'I see,' she said.

The constable began stuffing the garbage back into the sack. Mrs Upton watched him, giggling.

'If you haven't consumed all our stock of sherry, Mrs Upton,' said Mrs Julian, 'perhaps we might offer these two gentlemen a glass.'

The policemen, though on duty — which Mrs Julian had formerly supposed put the consumption of alcohol out of the question — took two glasses apiece. They were not at a loss for words and chatted away with Mrs Upton, possibly on the subject of the past and future exploits of Stewart. Mrs Julian scarcely listened and said nothing. She understood perfectly what had happened. Mr Arnold changing his clothes because they were wet, deciding to empty his rubbish that night because he had forgotten or failed to do so on the Saturday morning, gathering up his own and very likely Mr Laindon's too. At that point she had left the window to go to the telephone. In the few minutes during which she had been talking to her nephew, Mr Arnold had passed her gate with his barrow, lifted the lid of her dustbin and, finding a full sack within, taken it with him. It was this sack, her own, that she had seen him disposing of on the tip when she had next looked out.

No wonder the boiler had hardly ever been alight, no wonder the compost heap had scarcely grown. Once the snow and frost began and she knew her employer meant to remain indoors, Mrs Upton had abandoned the hygiene regimen and reverted to sack and dustbin. And this was what it had led to.

The two policemen left, obligingly discarding the sack on to the tip as they passed it. Mrs Upton looked at Mrs Julian and Mrs Julian looked at Mrs Upton and Mrs Upton said very brightly: "Well, I wonder what all that was about then?"

Mrs Julian longed and longed for the old days when she would have given her notice on the spot, but that was impossible now. Where would she find a replacement? So all she said was, knowing it to be incomprehensible: 'A faux pas, Mrs Upton, that's what it was,' and walked slowly off and into the living room where she picked up her knitting from the chair by the window and carried it into the furthest corner of the room.

As a detective she was a failure. Yet, ironically, it was directly due to her efforts that Mrs Arnold's murderer was brought to justice. Mrs Julian could not long keep away from her window and when she returned to it the next day it was to see the council men dismantling the tip and removing the sacks to some distant disposal unit or incinerator. As her newspaper had told her, the strike was over. But the hunt for the murder weapon was not. There was more room to manoeuvre and investigate now the rubbish was gone. By nightfall the weapon had been found and twenty-four hours later the young out-of-work mechanic who had struck Mrs Arnold down for the contents of her handbag had been arrested and charged.

They traced him through the spanner with which he had killed her and which, passing Mrs Julian's garden fence, he had thrust into the depths of her compost heap.

The Wrong Category

There hadn't been a killing now for a week. The evening paper's front page was devoted to the economic situation and an earthquake in Turkey. But page three kept up the interest in this series of murders. On it were photographs of the six victims all recognizably belonging to the same type. There, in every case although details of feature naturally varied, were the same large liquid eyes, full soft mouth, and long dark hair.

Barry's mother looked up from the paper. 'I don't like you going out at night.'

'What, me?' said Barry.

'Yes, you. All these murders happened round here. I don't like you going out after dark. It's not as if you had to, it's not as if it was for work.' She got up and began to clear the table but continued to speak in a low whining tone. 'I wouldn't say a word if you were a big chap. If you were the size of your cousin Ronnie I wouldn't say a word. A fellow your size doesn't stand a chance against that maniac.'

'I see,' said Barry. 'And whose fault is it I'm only five feet two? I might just point out that a woman of five feet that married a bloke only two inches more can't expect to have giants for kids. Right?'

'I sometimes think you only go roving about at night, doing what you want, to prove you're as big a man as your cousin Ronnie.'

Barry thrust his face close up to hers. 'Look, leave off, will you?' He waved the paper at her. 'I may not have the height but I'm not in the right category. Has that occurred to you? Has it?'

'All right, all right. I wish you wouldn't be always shouting.'

In his bedroom Barry put on his new velvet jacket and dabbed cologne on his wrists and neck. He looked spruce and dapper. His mother gave him an apprehensive glance as he passed her on his way to the back door, and returned to her contemplation of the pictures in the newspaper. Six of them in two months. The girlish faces, doe-eyed, diffident, looked back at her or looked aside or stared at distant unknown objects. After a while she folded the paper and switched on the television. Barry, after all, was not in the right category, and that must be her comfort.

He liked to go and look at the places where the bodies of the victims had been found. It brought him a thrill of danger and a sense of satisfaction. The first of them had been strangled very near his home on a path which first passed between draggled allotments, then became an alley plunging between the high brown wall of a convent and the lower red brick wall of a school.

Barry took this route to the livelier part of the town, walking rapidly but without fear and pausing at the point — a puddle of darkness between lamps — where the one they called Pat Leston had died. It seemed to him, as he stood there, that the very atmosphere, damp, dismal, and silent, breathed evil and the horror of the act. He appreciated it, inhaled it, and then passed on to seek, on the waste ground, the common, in a deserted back street of condemned houses, those other murder scenes. After the last killing they had closed the underpass, and Barry found to his disappointment that it was still closed.

He had walked a couple of miles and had hardly seen a soul. People stayed at home. There was even some kind of panic, he had noticed, when it got to six and the light was fading and the buses and tube trains were emptying themselves of the last commuters. In pairs they scurried. They left the town as depopulated as if a plague had scoured it.

Entering the High Street, walking its length, Barry saw no one, apart from those protected by the metal and glass of motor vehicles, but an old woman hunched on a step. Bundled in dirty clothes, a scarf over her head and a bottle in her hand, she was as safe as he — as far, or farther, from the right category.

But he was still on the watch. Next to viewing the spots where the six had died, he best enjoyed singling out the next victim. No one, for all the boasts of the newspapers and the policemen, knew the type as well as he did. Slight and small-boned, long-legged, sway-backed, with huge eyes, pointed features, and long dark hair. He was almost sure he had selected the Italian one as a potential victim some two weeks before the event, though he could never be certain.

So far today he had seen no one likely, in spite of watching with fascination the exit from the tube on his own way home. But now, as he entered the Red Lion and approached the bar, his eye fell on a candidate who corresponded to the type more completely than anyone he had yet singled out. Excitement stirred in him. But it was unwise, with everyone so alert and nervous, to be caught staring. The barman's eyes were on him. He asked for a half of lager, paid for it, tasted it, and, as the barman returned to rinsing glasses, turned slowly to appreciate to the full that slenderness, that soulful timid look, those big expressive eyes, and that mane of black hair.

But things had changed during the few seconds his back

had been turned. Previously he hadn't noticed that there were two people in the room, another as well as the candidate, and now they were sitting together. From intuition, at which Barry fancied himself as adept, he was sure the girl had picked the man up. There was something in the way she spoke as she lifted her full glass which convinced him, something in her look, shy yet provocative.

He heard her say, 'Well, thank you, but I didn't mean to. . .' and her voice trailed away, drowned by the other's brashness.

'Catch my eye? Think nothing of it, love. My pleasure. Your fella one of the unpunctual sort, is he?'

She made no reply. Barry was fascinated, compelled to stare, by the resemblance to Pat Leston, by more than that, by seeing in this face what seemed a quintessence, a gathering together and a concentrating here of every quality variously apparent in each of the six. And what gave it a particular piquancy was to see it side by side with such brutal ugliness. He wondered at the girl's nerve, her daring to make overtures. And now she was making them afresh, actually laying a hand on his sleeve.

'I suppose you've got a date yourself?' she said.

The man laughed. 'Afraid I have, love. I was just whiling away ten minutes.' He started to get up.

'Let me buy you a drink.'

His answer was only another harsh laugh. Without looking at the girl again, he walked away and through the swing doors out into the street. That people could expose themselves to such danger in the present climate of feeling intrigued Barry, his eyes now on the girl who was also leaving the pub. In a few seconds it was deserted, the only clients likely to visit it during that evening all gone.

A strange idea, with all its amazing possibilities, crossed his mind and he stood on the pavement, gazing the length of the High Street. But the girl had crossed the road and was waiting at the bus stop, while the man was only just visible in the distance, turning into the entrance of the underground car park.

Barry banished his idea, ridiculous perhaps and, to him, rather upsetting, and he crossed the road behind the on-coming bus wondering how to pass the rest of the evening. Review once more those murder scenes, was all that suggested itself to him and then go home.

It must have been the wrong bus for her. She was still waiting. And as Barry approached, she spoke to him, 'I saw you in the pub.'

'Yes,' he said. He never knew how to talk to girls. They intimidated and irritated him, especially when they were taller than he, and most of them were. The little thin ones he despised.

'I thought,' she said hesitantly, 'I thought I was going to have someone to see me home.'

Barry made no reply. She came out of the bus shelter, quite close to him, and he saw that she was much bigger and taller than he had thought at first.

'I must have just missed my bus. There won't be another for ten minutes.' She looked, and then he looked, at the shiny desert of this shopping centre, lighted and glittering and empty, pitted with the dark holes of doorways and passages. 'If you're going my way,' she said, 'I thought maybe. . .'

'I'm going through the path,' he said. Round there that was what everyone called it, the path.

'That'll do me.' She sounded eager and pleading. 'It's a short cut to my place. Is it all right if I walk along with you?'

'Suit yourself,' he said. 'One of them got killed down there. Doesn't that bother you?'

She only shrugged. They began to walk along together up the yellow and white glazed street, not talking, at least a yard apart. It was a chilly damp night, and a gust of wind caught them as, past the shops, they entered the path. The wind blew out the long red silk scarf she wore and she tucked it back inside her coat. Barry never wore a scarf, though most people did at this time of the year. It amused him to notice just how many did, as if they had never taken in the fact that all those six had been strangled with their own scarves.

There were lamps in this part of the path, attached by iron brackets to the red wall and the brown. Her sharp-featured face looked greenish in the light, and gaunt and scared. Suddenly he wasn't intimidated by her any more or afraid to talk to her.

'Most people,' he said, 'wouldn't walk down here at night for a million pounds.'

'You do,' she said. 'You were coming down here alone.'

'And no one gave me a million,' he said cockily. 'Look, that's where the first one died, just round this corner.'

She glanced at the spot expressionlessly and walked on ahead of Barry. He caught up with her. If she hadn't been wearing high heels she wouldn't have been that much taller than he. He pulled himself up to his full height, stretching his spine, as if effort and desire could make him as tall as his cousin Ronnie.

'I'm stronger than I look,' he said. 'A man's always stronger than a woman. It's the muscles.'

He might not have spoken for all the notice she took. The walls ended and gave place to low railings behind which the allotments, scrubby plots of cabbage stumps and waterlogged weeds, stretched away. Beyond them, but a long way off, rose the backs of tall houses hung with wooden balconies and iron staircases. A pale moon had come out and cast over this dismal prospect a thin cold radiance.

'There'll be someone killed here next,' he said. 'It's just the place. No one to see. The killer could get away over the allotments.'

She stopped and faced him. 'Don't you ever think about anything but those murders?'

'Crime interests me. I'd like to know why he does it.' He spoke insinuatingly, his resentment of her driven away by the attention she was at last giving him. 'Why d'you think he does it? It's not for money or sex. What's he got against them?'

'Maybe he hates them.' Her own words seemed to frighten her and, strangely, she pulled off the scarf which the wind had again been flapping, and thrust it into her coat pocket. 'I can understand that.' She looked at him with a mixture of dislike and fear. 'I hate men, so I can understand it,' she said, her voice trembling and shrill. 'Come on, let's walk.'

'No.' Barry put out his hand and touched her arm. His fingers clutched her coat sleeve. 'No, you can't just leave it there. If he hates them, why does he?'

'Perhaps he's been turned down too often,' she said backing away from him. 'Perhaps a long time ago one of them hurt him. He doesn't want to kill them but he can't help himself.' As she flung his hand off her arm the words came spitting out. 'Or he's just ugly. Or little, like you.'

Barry stood on tip-toe to bring himself to her height. He took a step towards her, his fists up. She backed against the railings and a long shudder went through her. Then she wheeled away and began to run, stumbling because her heels were high. It was those heels or the roughness of the ground or the new darkness as clouds dimmed the moon that brought her down.

Collapsed in a heap, one shoe kicked off, she slowly raised her head and looked up into Barry's eyes. He made no attempt to touch her. She struggled to her feet, wiped her grazed and bleeding hands on the scarf and immediately, without a word, they were locked together in the dark.

Several remarkable features distinguished this murder from the others. There was blood on the victim who had fair hair instead of dark, though otherwise strongly resembling Patrick Leston and Dino Facci. Apparently, since Barry

Halford had worn no scarf the murderer's own had been used. But ultimately it was the evidence of a slim dark-haired customer of the Red Lion which led the police to the conclusion that the killer of these seven young men was a woman.

About the Author

Ruth Rendell, whom the *Los Angeles Times* calls "the heiress apparent to Agatha Christie," is the author of MASTER OF THE MOOR, DEATH NOTES, THE SECRET HOUSE OF DEATH, TO FEAR A PAINTED DEVIL, A GUILTY THING SURPRISED, FROM DOON WITH DEATH, SINS OF THE FATHERS, WOLF TO THE SLAUGHTER, THE BEST MAN TO DIE, VANITY DIES HARD, and many other mysteries. She received the Current Crime Silver Cup Award for the best crime novel of 1976, the Crime Writers Association Gold Dagger for the best crime novel of 1975, and the Mystery Writers of America Edgar Award for the best short story of 1974. Ruth Rendell lives in a charming English village.